MOMENTS *of* LOVE, LUST *and* ECSTASY

LORNA RAMIREZ

Published in Australia by Lorna Ramirez

First published in Australia 2017

This edition published 2017

Copyright © Lorna Ramirez 2017

Cover design, typesetting: Working Type Studio, Melbourne

Cover photo: Dahiana Candelo, Unsplash.com

The right of Lorna Ramirez to be identified as the Author of the Work has been asserted in accordance with the Copyright, Designs and Patents Act 1988.

Ramirez, Lorna

Moments of Love, Lust & Ecstasy

ISBN: 978-0-646-97541-2

pp208

Acknowledgements

My special thanks to:

— Renalyn Cerezo, for typing my manuscript

— Alyssa Cary, my personal assistant

— the staff of Avondale Heights Library and Learning Centre, for helping me with my research.

Thanks for the support of:

— my loving husband, Claro

— my grandchildren, Alyssa and Amelia

— my children and their partners

— Carlo and Marie

— Maritess and Steve

— my sister, Victoria Polon.

Contents

Foreword

This book was written and is dedicated to those people who are suffering from mental illness due to tragic events that happened in their lives. This is the story of how the main character, Eliza, was able to pick up the pieces, start a new life and move on.

The book has sensitive issues that readers will find interesting and relatable. It is a must-read book for those who love romance, intrigue, drama and conflict. Perseverance, hope and the importance of setting goals and following one's dreams are all in this book.

The poems and inspirational messages are all written by me and are mostly excerpts from my two books, *My Innermost Thoughts* and *My Passion, My Calling*.

This is a fictional story and any similarities are all purely coincidental. It contains an open ending; I will let the readers explore their imaginations for what could happen.

Lorna Ramirez

Prologue

Eliza can feel a raging inferno engulfing her whole body. She can hardly breathe while preparing the table. It's a very special moment. She's waiting for Tony — her life, her love, her whole world — to arrive. Her dream of being with him for the rest of her life will now be a reality. Everything should be perfect: candles, table setting, music, the food she spent hours preparing.

Fully exhausted, Eliza pours her favourite white wine, then slumps into the sofa near the fireplace, slowly sipping. She starts to reminisce about her life, her past experiences, all leading up to where she is now.

She's so happy she's finally found her true happiness in life.

Chapter 1

Childhood

My name is Eliza Martinez, the youngest of the siblings of Mr and Mrs Enrique Martinez. I have two brothers, Jose and Carlo.

My father was a responsible, respected member of the community; a businessman, active in charity and the church. My mother was a stay at home mum, and of Spanish origin, while Dad is a pure Filipino — so I was blessed with beautiful features. Though we were well off, Dad insisted we still had to go to a public school, emphasising that wealth should not be a barrier in mixing with people of all walks of life.

We didn't live in one of the exclusive suburbs, but in one of the average residential areas in Quezon City, one of the cities that make up Metro Manila and the national capital of the Philippines.

I really loved my place — it was quiet and peaceful. Our house was one of the biggest in the area but our door was always open to visitors and people needing help. My dad had connections, hence he had the ability to help people, especially the disadvantaged.

At elementary and high school, I was popular not only for my beauty but my intelligence; I was the envy of many.

High school in the Philippines took only four years, then going to university would be 4–6 years depending on the course. I thoroughly enjoyed my high school years; I was very active in school days, with dancing and school debates. I was a popular student; all the boys in school were after me — but the only boy I did love was not in love with me. To him I didn't exist; he had a girlfriend, and though I tried to get his attention it seemed futile.

One day my best friend Lorna announced, "Hey Eliza, I have good news for you. Rudy is your leading man in the school play. Now you've got the chance to really know him."

"Wow, I can't wait for our rehearsal!" I answered.

That night I did not sleep properly. I keep tossing and turning, thinking of Rudy. He was in senior year (4th year) and I was in the junior year (3rd year).

After class, I went to the school hall and saw Rudy standing beside a table. My whole body shivered, especially when he smiled and held my hands. I was the lead character and Rudy was my boyfriend. It was a story of a feuding families but their children fell in love.

There was a scene where he kissed me on the cheek. I felt his lips and my tummy turned chaotic, as if hundreds of wild animals were trampling it.

We had several play rehearsals. The more I came to know him, the more I fell in love with him. He was such a gentleman, a caring and lovable person.

It was the last day of our rehearsal and the following day would be our end of year program presentation. Deep inside me, I wished it would never end.

While busy fixing my outfit, I heard Rudy call my name. "Eliza, you are a beautiful lady," he said. "Any man would be a fool not to admire your beauty, your intelligence and personality. I do like you, but only as a friend. I do love someone and I am faithful and committed to her. I am sorry. I don't want to hurt your feelings or break your heart."

Quite embarrassed I asked, "Rudy, you know? Did Lorna mention it?"

"No one did," Rudy explained. "I could feel it at the start. Can we still be friends?"

"Sure," I replied. "No hard feelings. I do understand."

I cried myself to sleep that night, asking myself why it happened to me. I had so many admirers and yet someone I loved so much didn't love me. This was not fair.

The following day was an important day at the school. It was the year-end presentation program. The play was a complete success, a standout at the program. After the show, Rudy came to shake my hand and said goodbye — I was so heartbroken.

When vacation came, I missed my school and Rudy most of all. I knew I had to get used to the idea that I wouldn't be seeing Rudy anymore!

High school started later, part of the last Monday of June. I was now in my final year (4th year), graduating next year and then to university.

Without Rudy, I concentrated more on my studies, still active in school activities. As always, lots of boys were after me but I was not interested in any of them. Rudy was always on my mind. Where was he? What was he doing now?

My parents were very proud on the day of our graduation. I was the salutatorian (2nd place) of the graduating class of 1970.

After the graduation ceremony, we had a graduation dance ball. I did not have any partner at the ball, refusing all invitations, not interested at all in any boy!

Friends that last forever
And loving families
These are priceless
Worth more than the riches of the world
They give us the reason
That life is worth living

— From *My Innermost Thoughts*
by Lorna Ramirez

Chapter 2

The Ordeal

University was very different compared to high school. I found new freedom, with no one telling me what to do. It was up to me to shape my future.

I enrolled at the oldest university in the Philippines, the University of Santo Tomas, taking up a four year course in journalism, media and communications. For me this was a perfect course, as I loved writing and meeting people. As always I was very active in school, joining the university sorority and the student writing class in the university paper.

Through my course I came to know different kinds of people, and had lots of admirers and suitors; but no one could fill the gap Rudy left in my heart. I still yearned for his love.

Four years passed, and in 1974 I was now in my last year of my course, looking forward to graduating in about a month's time and be working in a newspaper, or probably in media and television — that was my ultimate goal.

As a member of a sorority in our school, we would be having a two day seminar on the outskirts of Manila. I asked my brother Jose to pick me up after school Friday afternoon and drop me off at Tagaytay for our seminar. I packed everything that night for the two days.

March and April in Manila were so hot and steamy. I was outside the school gate waiting for my brother but instead I saw Freddie, one of his friends. Freddie belonged to a wealthy family; his father owned several big business ventures in Manila. With enthusiasm, Freddie said, "C'mon Eliza, your brother asked me to pick you up and drop you off at the seminar."

"Is that so? Okay, thanks." I got inside the car. "This is a nice car, Freddie. Must be new?"

Freddie boasted, "Oh yeah! Dad bought it as my birthday gift. By the way, which hotel are you booked at in Tagaytay, Eliza?"

"Taal Vista Hotel."

"It's a nice hotel," Freddie commented.

"Yes, all of our sorority members will be staying there and a big function will be this Sunday."

Tagaytay City, in the province of Cavite, is a major tourist spot and only 55 kilometres from the city of Manila. It overlooks Taal Lake in Batangas and provide a view of Taal Island, a volcano in the middle of a lake.

We had been travelling for an hour; I was getting quite restless. I had been to Tagaytay with my family a few times and I was not familiar with the surroundings. I said with my heart beating fast, "Freddie, is this the best way to Tagaytay?"

Freddie replied, "We will be passing Tagaytay and driving into Nasugbu, Batangas to meet some friends, then we'll be heading your way."

The western part of Nasugbu, Batangas is famous for beach resorts. Along the national highway, one could see fields of sugar cane, corn and rice against hills and mountain. It is about 102 km from metro Manila.

My heart was pounding in my chest, I was terrified. All I could see were rice fields, hills and mountains. I begin to panic and screamed, "Where are you taking me, Freddie?"

"Shut up, you have to wait and see," Freddie shouted.

Then we stopped in the middle of the rice field and I could see a small, decent house. Freddie knocked and the door opened. Inside I could see three of his friends smiling eagerly, staring at me — ready to attack me. One of them said, "Is this our meal for tonight?"

Freddie, smiling, said, "It is our dessert for tonight."

I screamed and cried, "Freddie, what are you talking about? Please don't hurt me. Let me go, I beg you."

"No way Eliza, a few times you snubbed me and this is the price you pay for that," Freddie warned.

I knew then I was in a very bad situation. No one could hear me scream in this place. It was in the middle of nowhere. Tears flowed down my cheeks.

"It's no use screaming, reserve your strength for the rest of the day. No one can hear you. You are at our mercy," Freddie said. "Eliza, listen carefully. If you tell anyone about this, your brother and father will be killed. I've got connections and I really mean it."

We went inside the house. We were in the lounge room when Freddie yelled, "Eliza, undress slowly and dance."

One of his friends turned on the phonograph and played soft, sexy music.

With an evil look Freddie said, "C'mon Eliza, entertain us, we want to be excited and thrilled by your performance. Do it slowly, inviting and with passion."

They all surrounded me, eagerly waiting the show I had to do.

Tears flowing, I slowly undressed myself, closing my eyes — I didn't want to see their disgusting faces. All I could hear was laughter, moaning and obscene remarks. Then I was fully naked; that's when Freddie grabbed my behind, forcing me to the bedroom, the three friends following. Freddie pushed me to the bed and went on top of me. I could smell alcohol on his breath. My body froze, I became numb. I was a virgin and Freddie had the satisfaction of deflowering me!

He begun thrusting backwards and forwards. Then I felt a heavy syrupy liquid coming out between my legs. I tried to scream but no voice came out. The three friends in the room all watched with delight, like animals, waiting for their turns.

I passed out, to be awoken when a glass of water was poured onto my face. Back to my senses, and another guy was on top of me, doing the same rhythmic movement. I felt desecrated, passing out a few times, each time being revived.

The last time they revived me, I felt a penis inside my mouth, while hearing them screaming, laughing and saying, "Suck it hard baby or we will slash your throat."

The ordeal lasted for several hours until I felt that I'd already died, wishing they wouldn't be able to revive me.

After the ordeal, they locked me in the bedroom, tying my hands on each side of my bed. I was still naked and a blanket was put on top of me.

I cried and cried and wished I'd died already. I felt intense pain around my privates and throughout my whole body. I felt dirty and violated.

From the bedroom I could hear their laughter and how they enjoyed the sex. I was furious but had no choice but to be calm.

Because of the ordeal, I fell asleep and only woke up the following day when Freddie untied me and said, "Clean up yourself first. Have a shower then I will give you your breakfast. After that, I will drive you to Taal Vista Hotel for your sorority seminar. Don't say a word of what happened or else I will kill both your brother and father."

I had my shower and cleaned myself. It was now Saturday morning; the seminar would start at 10.00 am.

"Here is your breakfast. My friends are all gone. I am ready now to drop you off in Tagaytay," Freddie said.

"I don't have the appetite to eat. Just drive me to my destination," I suggested.

It was a beautiful Saturday morning. Freddie started driving, I was very quiet. Then Freddie reminded me again: "I know you can get a ride back home, your brother told me. Remember what I said? No one should ever know what happened."

Arriving at the hotel around 9.00 am, I quickly registered at the lobby. I saw a few of my friends, whom asked why I did not arrive Friday night. One of them even commented that I looked haggard and sick.

I did not give an explanation and just said, "What's important is that I finally made it."

The seminar would last for Saturday and Sunday, and a grand finale with dance music would be on Sunday night. Most of my sorority sisters brought their friends, boyfriends and husbands.

Thoroughly enjoying our seminar, for a while I forgot the ordeal I had been through. However, a few of my friends began to notice the change within. I used to be the bubbly type, full of life and energy — but for those two days, I was quite subdued and sad. I told them that I was feeling sick and probably beginning to get a flu or virus.

Sunday night was the finale, with dancing, lots of food and award presentations. It was a complete success, lasting almost to 2.00 am. The following day, all of us were packing to go home. One of my friends offered me a ride. Their place was just a few kilometres from my home. What a nice feeling to be home again!

So much pain and sorrow I feel
Like a sword or dagger
Slowly piercing through my heart
Dissecting it into pieces
At times I feel I've already
Died a thousand times
Each time bouncing
Back again to life
To face once more
Anguish and heartache
Fighting back as much as I can
Please help me God

—Lorna Ramirez

Chapter 3

Trauma

The housemaid opened the gate, thanking my friend for giving me a lift. I went inside our house hurriedly and saw Mum in the lounge room.

"Glad to see you, Eliza. How was your seminar? Did you have a good time?" Mum asked.

"Yes I did, but I feel exhausted — I just want to go straight to my room and rest."

"Okay, but if you're ready, I cooked your favourite dish, kare-kare."

'Kare-kare' is a popular Pilipino dish: a beef stew boiled in peanut sauce with different vegetables, eggplant, beans and bok choy.

I stayed in my room for the rest of the day and slept, only woken by Mum knocking on my door. "Are you feeling okay? You didn't eat your lunch and it's almost dinner time.

Please prepare yourself, get ready for dinner. Your dad's just arrived from a business trip and he's looking for you."

"Okay Mum. I'll be down in a minute. We had such hectic days at the seminar, and I'm still exhausted."

At dinner, I was quiet but so relieved and happy I was with my family.

"It was so kind of Freddie volunteering to drive you to Tagaytay," Jose mentioned.

"What? I thought you would be the one to drive her to Tagaytay. Why did you let someone take charge of my little girl?" Dad accused Jose.

Jose explained. "Dad, I did have a prior commitment. What is important is that she is here now, safe and sound."

Trying to control myself, I remained calm. I could hardly breathe or swallow my food.

"What's wrong Eliza? You barely touched your food!" Mum said.

"I think I'm getting the flu or a virus, not really feeling well."

"He he." Jose smiled. "It's only exhaustion and hangover. Did you have a lot to drink at the party?"

My other brother Carlo quickly replied, "Yeah Eliza, you look sick. You don't want to be sick, your graduation will be next month."

Usually after dinner, the whole family sat in the lounge

room, and at times (depending on my mood) I played the piano. Carlo would be singing — he had a good voice. But most of the time, we just talked about what we did for the day. Lately, we seldom had our dinner together. Dad at times would be on a business trip. My two brothers would be with friends, and I was busy with schoolwork and school functions.

We were a very close-knit family. Dad, being the head of the family, was a strict yet very caring person and a good provider, always there to help us with our problems. The only difference was that this time, I couldn't tell him of my own predicament.

"Guys, I have to go to my room now. So sorry I can't join you tonight."

I went straight to my room. I cried and cried. Tuesday morning I did not go to my classes; I stayed in bed for the whole day, skipping breakfast, lunch and dinner. Both my parents were worried.

"You haven't eaten for the whole day. Both your dad and I are really worried. How can we help?" Mum asked.

"It's okay Mum. I'm just exhausted."

That night, I had a nightmare, screaming in my sleep. My parents rushed to my room, wondering what was happening.

"Eliza, please help us to help you. What happened at the seminar?" both my parents pleaded.

"Nothing Dad. I do believe I'm just feeling exhausted, probably burned out from schoolwork, activities, and the coming graduation. Also, I think I'm coming down with a virus."

I couldn't look at my parents' eyes. I felt dirty, thinking I wasn't worthy now to be their daughter.

My nightmares and flashbacks, continuous for several days, was the reason for my parents insisting that I should see our family doctor.

"I will be away for a business trip to Hong Kong, Eliza. And I want to be sure everything is okay. I will ring up our family doctor and he'll be here tonight to see you. Just before your graduation next month, I will be back," my dad promised.

"Nice of you Dad," I said.

Our family doctor came that night. I told my parents I needed privacy; they understood and willingly left my room.

"Tell me how you feel, Eliza. Your blood pressure is a bit below normal but not a concern this time. You have heart palpitations — you're probably anxious and upset. You look stressed and agitated. What happened?" he asked.

I was reluctant at first, then I finally agreed and confessed. "It's an ordeal that my parents are not supposed to know. I had been threatened." Then I burst into tears. "Doc, I was gang-raped."

"Do you want to press charges? I can testify," our family doctor suggested.

"No Doc! It would create more problems. I do hope you won't tell my parents about my ordeal."

"Of course not, Eliza! For now I will take a blood sample for full analysis. I will also prescribe you sleeping pills and antidepressants. These should be taken only for a short term. I am sure, with the full support of your family, you can deal with your depression."

"I will do my best, Doc. Thanks."

When our family doctor came out, Mum and Dad eagerly asked about my condition. "What's wrong with my little girl, Doc?"

"She is suffering from depression. Stress from school. At times it just happens at a stage in our lives, predominantly for overachievers like Eliza."

"But what about her nightmares?" Dad anxiously asked.

"I gave her pills. They will disappear slowly. Please be gentle and understanding. It's all that she needs. She got inner conflicts and she is the only one who can resolve them."

"We will do our very best to help her. We love her dearly. And thanks Doc," my dad said.

The next day, Dad would be leaving for a business trip to Hong Kong. But before leaving, he went in my room, hugged and kissed me and said, "Please be strong, Eliza. Whatever your problems are, your mum and dad will always be here for you."

Mum brought meals to my bedroom, doing the same routine for almost two weeks. Oftentimes Dad rang and a few times I talked to him.

I did not attend my classes for almost two weeks, so it was lucky I had finished all my exams, school projects and the requirements for our graduation before the ordeal happened.

One day Mum knocked on my door. "Your friends are here, Lynda and Evelyn. They want to see you."

"Please tell them I'm quite okay now but I'm not ready yet to see them."

"I will do that. By the way Eliza, your brother Jose wants to talk to you. Will I let him in?"

"Yes please."

Jose entered my room and asked with concern, "What's wrong Eliza? Since you came back from the seminar, you're acting weird. You refrain from seeing people, not attending your classes. Was there anything that I should know that happened when Freddie drove you to the seminar?"

I started feeling uneasy. Then I uttered, "This has nothing to do with Freddie."

Jose believed me. "I tried reaching Freddie to ask what happened and ..."

I interrupted Jose. "And ... what did he say?"

"I wasn't able to reach him. His parents said he left for America to continue his studies," Jose added.

I sighed with relief. "As I said before, this has got nothing to do with Freddie. My resistance weakened because of too many school activities, and the coming graduation. I just need a break and rest."

"Be strong sis, try to recover soon. Your big day is coming!"

Thanks to my family doctor's prescriptions of sleeping pills and antidepressants, I was slowly recovering. Our family doctor rang up, informing us all blood test results were normal.

True to his promise, in about two and a half weeks, just before graduation, Dad came back. He went straight to my room and said, "How are you, my little girl?"

"Slowly recovering, Dad. Thanks to the family support and the medication, I am on the road to recovery."

"That's my girl. I don't want to ask you again. You are entitled to your own privacy but when the time comes, if you decide to tell us we will always be here to support you."

"Thanks Dad."

Each of us has a cross to carry
Each of us will go through trying times in our lives
But with our faith, our trust in Him
And with the support of families and friends
The crosses will be bearable
To carry throughout our journey in life!

From *My Innermost Thoughts*
by Lorna Ramirez

Chapter 4
Recovery

I slowly regained my appetite and tried to cut down on my medication. It was more than a month since my ordeal and I was determined to put aside the past and move on. It wasn't fair for my family to see me going downhill. They loved me so much and would do everything for me. My family was my inspiration to achieve my dream of becoming a successful journalist and writer.

I started reading my favourite books, playing classical pieces and going out into the garden, especially in the morning. I could feel the warmth of the sun on my face, the wind slowly caressing my hair. I enjoyed the fragrance of roses and jasmine. At last I felt free and alive. Freddie was now in America. I wouldn't be seeing him, reminding me of my ordeal.

Linda, Evelyn and some of my university friends visited me. I talked to them. They were so happy for my progress.

My weight slowly came back; I lost 7 kilos. Of course both my parents were elated.

The big day finally came, my graduation. I was the 'summa cum laude', the highest honour in my Bachelor of Arts majoring in Journalism. My parents were so proud of me. I still looked frail and pale, but otherwise feeling fine. All of my friends were so happy to see me and congratulated me for my achievement.

I made a valedictory speech, delivering the closing and farewell statement at the graduation ceremony. Most of my friends said it was short and simple but impressive.

After the ceremony, Dad said, "Okay, we will be heading straight home."

My brother Carlo insisted, "Are we not going to a restaurant? To celebrate the occasion?"

"No Carlo, your sister will need rest so we are heading home."

It was quite unusual for Dad to decide not to celebrate my achievement. I started to have doubts. Was it because of the pain and sorrow I had given them? I felt a bit disappointed.

It was around 10.00 pm when we arrived home. The house and front yard were in total darkness. I even told Dad that maybe we had a blackout or an electrical problem. As we walked inside, *boom!* The house was fully lit and lots of friends even my high school friends were there!

"Ladies and gentlemen, presenting to you our pride and joy and my only daughter … Eliza," Dad said, beaming with pride.

There was lots of food and dancing. My friends from the university came and joined the celebration.

"You all tricked me," I said, "I never expected this!"

"You thank Jose, your brother, doing the hard work to make it a success," said Dad.

"How come I didn't know about this? Well, being the middle sibling, I'm not important," Carlo complained.

"C'mon Carlo, you are one of the most important people in my life. Now my dear brother Jose, Thank you so much for everything."

"Sis, I will do anything for you!"

I realised that so many people did love me, I wouldn't disappoint them. I had to bury the past and move on!

I decided to take a few more months before looking for a job. My family suggested that we take a short vacation in Tagaytay for a few days. I refused and said, "I don't want to travel — I prefer staying home."

They all agreed.

After four months of complete rest, I was back to my normal weight. And I started looking for a job.

Then Dad said, "By the way Eliza, there is an assistant reporter position open in one of the leading newspapers.

You can apply for that. I won't help — you have to apply on your own merit."

"Of course, Dad, I won't ask for your help."

I made several job applications to newspapers, and other media such as television and radio companies. I got several replies, interviews and job offers. I decided to take the position of an assistant reporter in a newspaper. I was looking forward to starting my first job in about three weeks' time.

On Monday morning, my first day of work, I got up early and said to myself, "This is it! A new beginning in my life." I felt blessed and lucky. One blessing was I did not get pregnant after my ordeal, and that made my life a lot easier.

Mum woke up early too, making sure our house help prepared a nice full breakfast for me. After my breakfast, Mum walked me to the door and said, "Sweetie, good luck on your job!"

"Thanks Mum."

At work, I went straight to the office of Mr Daniel Chavez, the head of the department. He was tall and quite good-looking, serious but with an impressive personality.

"Welcome to the team!" Danny said.

"Thanks, Mr Chavez."

"Just call me Danny. We're an informal team, we use

first names. But we work hard, with long hours needed at times, especially when we're covering an important story. A tough job but rewarding. Tomorrow, I will orient you on what we're doing."

Danny then called in one of the team members. "Hi Eliza. I'm Mira," she said, "I will show you your desk, introduce you to our team members and tour you around our office."

It was a busy office, all paperwork and telephones ringing.

"Here is your desk, Eliza. You are in front of Danny's office. Unfortunately the boys are out, Sammy and Joe are doing interviews."

Mira was really friendly, showing me where I could get stationery supplies, the ladies' toilet, the library and so on. She introduced me to Terry, Vicky and Edna, our team members. After the orientation, I went back to my desk, where Mira handed me my job responsibilities and descriptions. I also had to read the company rules and regulations.

I carefully read my job description, absorbing the details of what I'd be doing as an assistant reporter. Time went by so fast, I did not realise it was lunch time until Mira called out, "Eliza, We'll go to the cafeteria. Terry, Vicky, Edna and I think the boys, Sammy and Joe, will all be there."

The cafeteria was in the first floor. A nice cafeteria, with a variety of food to choose from. Our team sat near the window.

"Eliza, this is Sammy, our photographer. And Joe, our reporter. You already met Terry, Vicky and Edna."

"Nice to meet you all."

"We heard that you graduated summa cum laude in your class. You must be very smart," Terry inquired.

"Well, not really, just hard work."

"You're just being humble," Vicky said.

"Hey Eliza," Mira said laughing, "Do you know that our own boss, Danny, is still single? Very available. Such a pity, a good-looking guy with no time for love. Well, I suppose he is married to his job. Maybe you can change his mind, Eliza."

They all laughed, and Vicky said, "It's only a joke Eliza, but no one knows — it might happen."

As an assistant reporter, I played an active part in gathering information on all aspects of investigations before a story could be produced in the paper. It was very hectic and stressful work and I had to meet strict deadlines.

I knew this was what I wanted to be — busy, and hence forgetting all the bad experiences I had been through.

My family was ecstatic and proud of my progress. They could see a complete transformation within me. At the dinner table, Dad commented, "So happy for you, Eliza. I know you can be a successful reporter."

"Thanks Dad. The truth is, it's all my family support and love that helps me overcome everything. Actually, I got a wonderful and friendly team. But my boss Danny is quite serious, very formal. I could deal with that."

"I know you can do your work well, Eliza. I believe in you!"

"Thanks Mum."

On Tuesday morning, Danny started briefing me on the things we would be doing for the next few weeks. "As reporters, we should be flexible in our working hours. At times we work past midnight, especially when we're following up a story. This work demands long hours, irregular schedules and some travel."

"I'm okay with that, Danny."

"That's good. This is the first case you will be involved in. A known TV personality was gang-raped. You do know the case of the actress Maggie de la Riva? It's similar to that."

My face went white. I nearly choked.

"What's wrong Eliza? You look shocked! Don't worry, you won't be involved in field work. You will be in the office collecting and compiling all information supplied by your team. As you gain experience, you will be involved in the field," Danny explained.

In our department, the team handled reports of crimes committed and sometimes political issues as well. I was confident I could deal with all of these!

Doing this case, I could prove I can face my fear courageously — an ultimate challenge, overcoming triumphantly any doubt within me.

Months passed. Danny started noticing that I worked hard, most times staying back late. A lot of times I rejected my workmates' invitations to clubs and parties.

"You don't have to kill yourself working, Eliza. Have fun! You're still young. Don't be like me," Danny said.

"I'm not really into that thing, Danny. I do like working and I enjoy it."

Danny and I had something in common: we loved our work. We shared the same passion. We were the centre of jokes within our team. I just ignored them.

A year and a half passed. I was promoted as a senior reporter; it was a quick promotion but no one complained. All of them realised my potential and capabilities. I was now in line next to Danny. We spent so much time together, I felt we were getting closer and closer, and it really scared me. I wasn't ready for any romantic relationship with any guy, not even Danny.

One Friday afternoon, everybody was rushing home but our team would go for a drink or two to celebrate Mira's birthday.

"C'mon Eliza, we'll be going out for a drink," Mira said.

"So sorry Mira, I'm rushing this report. I have to give this to Danny first thing in the morning. I'm sure you won't be offended if I won't go. Anyway, I came out with you for lunch so I will pass this time."

"Not a problem. You and Danny are so much alike. You two should get married. Match made in heaven." She laughed.

"Here we go again. That does not even cross my mind."

"Only kidding, Eliza. Don't be upset. Good night."

"I know. Good night Mira."

Just past 8.00 pm I was about to leave, then Danny came to my desk and said, "Can I talk to you Eliza?"

"Oh Danny, I'm already finished with my project and ready to give it to you first thing in the morning."

"It's not about work, Eliza. It's something else."

I was a bit surprised. "What?"

"I don't know where to start. I'm afraid I am falling in love with you. This is the first time I've felt this way since my breakup with a girl eight years ago."

I was not expecting this. Deep inside I did like him but it was still too early for me to have a romantic attachment. "I'm so flattered Danny, but please understand, I'm not ready to have any relationship yet."

"Why Eliza? Just because a guy broke your heart, you

won't give yourself a chance to love and find the bliss of being loved? It's not fair for you and for me. Please let me show you how to love and be loved again."

"It's so complicated, Danny. I do like you but as a friend. I'm sorry, I'm not ready yet."

There was a complete silence for a moment.

"I respect your decision, Eliza. But if you change your mind, I will always be here."

"Thanks Danny, I'm pretty sure I won't change my mind."

When Danny tried to give me a friendly hug, I panicked, my body froze and I screamed. "What's wrong, Eliza? I won't hurt you. It's just a friendly hug."

"Nothing Danny. It's just me — rekindled memories from the past. Please don't ask any more. Good night."

"Good night Eliza."

I didn't have a proper sleep that night. I had a soft spot for him. He was kind and mature, ten years older than me. A perfect person for a perfect relationship. But it would be unfair for him that I was still unstable, emotionally and sexually, and not ready for a romantic relationship.

We remained friends and after two and a half years, Danny was promoted to a senior management level. I took his position as the head of the department.

With my strong faith in Him
Plus the love and support of
My families and friends I know
I can get through all the
Challenges I face
As I walk through the journey of life.

From *My Innermost Thoughts*

by Lorna Ramirez

Chapter 5

Australia

I saw Danny every now and then at the office, but never
really had a chance to talk to him. We just said hello
with a smile. Still the same — Danny married to his job.

As the head of the department, I tried my best to be fair
to everyone, while remaining strict and firm when it came
to work schedules and deadlines. I was open-minded to all
ideas and suggestions from my team members, encouraging and motivating them to be the best they could be. Each
of them was an efficient and effective team player. Because
of this, our department was awarded as the 'best' in the
national newspaper awards.

One Sunday afternoon, a friend of the family visited
us, Mrs Leony Lopez. I called her Auntie Leony. She was
so excited, telling us that her family would be migrating to Australia. She informed us that immigration was

now open in Australia and encouraged me to apply. Dad replied, "That's a good idea, Eliza. Who knows, you might be successful in Australia."

I quickly answered, "I'll think it over."

The next day, without informing my family I left work early to go to the Australian embassy. I got an application form, filled it out and sent it.

I forget all about it until after four months, I received a letter from the embassy. I told my parents that my application was being considered, but I had to submit documents, attend interviews and submit to a physical exam. Beaming, my dad said, "So happy for you, it's the right decision. By the way, choose Melbourne as your destination — I will get in touch with the Rosales family. You know them, they were our neighbours. They have an only daughter, Celia, four years older than you."

"Of course Dad, I do remember."

"Good, I will get in touch with them. They always send us a Christmas card each year. At least you'll have someone helping you while you are still searching in Australia."

'Thanks a lot Dad."

I continued working, but taking leave in between other stuff. Mira asked, "You've been taking leave lately, is there something we should know?"

I laughed and responded, "No, I just have to attend to

some personal things. If anything happens, our team will be the first to know."

I passed all the requirements, being granted a visa and a permanent residency. The following day, I submitted my letter of resignation and called a meeting in my department. They were all sad to see me go, but also happy and wished me success in my new journey.

At the cafeteria, I was having my lunch when Danny came. I saw sadness on his face. He inquired, "I heard the news, is it true? I'm so happy for you. May you find happiness and success ... I will be missing you so much. You'll be forever in my mind." He shook my hand and then said goodbye.

For the next two months, I was busy at work training Mira as my replacement. On my last day of work we all went for a farewell lunch. My staff gave me a nice pen and a beautiful cross pendant. That moment I was carried away and tears started flowing. I felt a lump in my throat and was speechless. That moment I had doubts if I made the right decision. But I had to take the risk. Going to Australia would be the only way to forget my trauma. This would be a new beginning and new life for me.

My family were ecstatic, but sad — especially my two brothers, Carlo and Jose. Both Mum and Dad reminded me, "Eliza, if you find it difficult to adjust to settle in

Australia, don't hesitate to come back. We will welcome you with open arms."

I said, "Don't worry, I'm sure it will work fine for me. Of course, once settled I will always come back and visit you." I was really looking forward to my new life in Australia.

As my departure date got closer, I started to have sleepless nights; restlessness and sadness filled my heart. I would miss my beautiful supportive family who had helped me overcome the darkest moments of my life. I would miss my staff and friends at work.

September 25, 1977: The day of my departure. My flight was at 9.00 pm. All my family was there: my parents, Jose and Carlo. My workmates were also there, including Danny. I could feel his anguish and sorrow, and a melancholy tone in his voice as he said with sadness, "Please remember Eliza, my proposal is still open. I will be waiting in case you change your mind."

I cut him off quickly and replied, "Look Danny, don't be hard on yourself. This is not fair for you. So sorry, I made my decision. I'm not ready for a relationship with anyone. Goodbye."

Then I gave Danny a light kiss on his cheek, much to his surprise. He held my hands solemnly and said, "I wish you all success and I'm sure you'll be able to achieve all your goals and dreams. Goodbye Eliza!"

"Thanks Danny."

When it was time to go inside the departure area, I hugged Mum and Dad. Tears flowed from my parents' eyes. Mum started to cry and Dad hugged her; it was a very sad scene and Dad spoke with tenderness to my mother. "This is good for our little girl. Let her discover herself. I have faith in her. She can do this."

I hugged my brothers with tears in my eyes. Jose said, "Please visit us soon, sister. We will be missing you, especially your generous smile."

I walked fast, almost running. I didn't want to look back or else I would come running back to them. I could hardly breathe; I felt a sword piercing through my heart, slowly cutting it into pieces. But I managed to pull through, composing myself as I went inside the departure area. This was the first time I was away from my family. It was very hard for me and my family to adjust to this situation.

I took the night flight, eight hours' travel from Manila to Australia. I couldn't sleep for the entire flight, still wondering if I made the right decision. I had a nice, loving, supportive family and a successful career, and now I was going to another country with no family and friends. Was this the right move?

It was spring in Australia. I thought it would still be cold. We landed at the Melbourne Airport around 9.00 am. After going through customs I headed to the arrival exit door and saw the Rosales family. They were delighted to see me. "Hi Auntie Nelly and Uncle Chris, so happy to be here in Australia."

"Gosh Eliza," Auntie Nelly said, "you are a pretty and a gorgeous lady. You remember Celia? She's still with us — single, too busy with her job. I'm still waiting for my grandkids!"

Celia explained, "I have not met the right person yet Mum, please stop putting pressure on me. Anyway Eliza, we used to play together remember?"

"Of course I do, you always teased me and made me cry!"

"C'mon guys, we have to go now. Eliza needs rest," my uncle Chris suggested.

While inside the car, both Mr and Mrs Rosales assured me that I would love Australia and I made the right decision. They lived in the northern suburb of Essendon. From the airport to their place, I was overwhelmed by what I saw. Big open spaces, fresh air and everything seemed so clean.

We arrived at their place around 11.10 am. It was a big house for a family of three, with four bedrooms, lounge, family room and a spacious kitchen.

"Feel at home Eliza, you can stay as long as you want," said Auntie Nelly. "Once you're settled and have a secure job, you'll probably want a place of your own — whatever suits you Eliza, we are here to help."

I felt really welcome and already a part of the family. I said, "Thanks Auntie Nelly, for your generosity and support."

"Mum, Dad,' Celia said with enthusiasm, 'I have taken two weeks of leave. I will help Eliza get her Medicare card, and I can show her around Melbourne."

"Thanks to all of you, you are all so kind."

"I will show your room, Eliza, have a rest. Then we'll all be having a late lunch," Auntie Nelly offered.

I got a nice, decent sized room. While carefully arranging all my things, I thought I would be enjoying my stay in Australia.

I applied for the overseas qualification for my degree. I was so lucky that the University of Santo Tomas was one of the few universities from the Philippines that were recognised. After a few weeks my document arrived, granting me an accredited level for my Bachelor of Arts, Major in Journalism.

Wasting no time, I applied for several positions related to my course. Unfortunately, without local experience I found it difficult to find a job.

Celia suggested I be prepared to apply for a lower position. "Just to get in and gain experience, eventually you'll be able to get your dream job."

Celia was a successful industrial chemist, a laboratory manager in a big oil company. She was very dedicated to her job, often going overseas and interstate for conferences and other assignments.

After almost five months and hundreds of job applications, there was finally a success. One of Melbourne's leading newspapers rang, wanting to interview me for the position of a customer service clerk: not the kind of job I wanted, but I was desperate.

There were three people in the interview room. I was feeling so nervous but I answered all their questions with flying colours. It lasted for almost an hour; after that, they told me that they'd get in touch with me ASAP.

I was so exhausted when I arrived at my place. Auntie Nelly was busy cooking lamb shanks. Celia would be arriving that night from a work conference in Singapore. Upon seeing me, Auntie Nelly eagerly asked me about my interview. With reluctance I commented, "I think I did well but still not sure if I'll be getting the job."

It was a long, nail-biting week for me, then I received a letter saying I got the job. I jumped with joy; Celia heard me screaming (she wasn't working that day) and came out of her room. "What's wrong Eliza? You're spastic!"

I answered, "I got the job!"

Celia was also happy, and gave me a tight hug. My whole body froze and started shaking. Celia was bewildered. "What's wrong Eliza? You're shaking!"

"There's nothing wrong. Celia. I'm just not used to being hugged by anyone other than my family."

Celia said, "Sorry Eliza, I promise not to do it again."

Straight away I called my parents to tell them of the good news. Of course they were so happy.

It's up to us to relinquish the past
Then let it go and move on
Failing to do so
We become a prisoner of ourselves
And peace within
Can never be found

From *My Passion, My Calling* by Lorna Ramirez

Chapter 6

Love or Lust

I t was summertime in Australia and I loved the weather. It was a perfect season for my first job; no cold morning to go to work. It was Monday February 27th in 1978, a very special day for me: my first day of work. I woke up early, cheerful and in a good mood. Auntie Nelly was already awake and wished me good luck for my first job.

I arrived at the office quite early. I was the first one at our department; only the cleaners were at the building. Then at 8.45am, other employees started coming.

I met my supervisor David, a tall good-looking man. He quickly briefed me on my job responsibilities and Tina, the team leader, toured me around the place. The department had the same atmosphere and environment as back home: busy and chaotic.

They were all friendly, knowing that I was relatively

new in the country. All were very supportive and helpful. We were six people in our section: Sue, Tina, Martin, Marie, myself and the supervisor David.

As a customer service clerk I would be responsible for all paperwork and customer complaints, occasionally helping the reporters do their research. Except for David we were all young, hence I could relate to all of them.

Within the next few months, I adjusted to the new environment, much to the surprise and delight of my supervisor and workmates.

Most Friday evenings I went out with them for a drink or two, once in a while night clubbing and just having fun.

I enrolled for driving lessons during weekends. Celia patiently helped me to practise driving. After my practice, we went shopping and to the cinema; if we had time, we also went on long drives around the outskirts of Melbourne. Celia also took me to different vineyards within Victoria.

Already loving Australia, my newfound friends and most of all my freedom, slowly I began to forget my ordeal and trauma. Celia was so caring, supportive and helpful. There were moments when I wondered why she was doing all this. But I could feel safe with Celia's family.

There were quite a few men who tried to win my heart, but I ignored them. Probably in time I would meet someone who could sweep me off my feet. It wasn't the right time for me to be involved with anyone.

A year passed. I was still living the Rosales family, trying to save as much as I could to have my own flat. I made once monthly long distance calls to my family to alleviate my feelings of loneliness, having not seen them for almost a year now.

In the first week of November 1978, Auntie Nelly broke news. "Your dad and I will be having a three month around the world tour. This is our dream holiday. I'm sure both of you will be okay."

"Of course," Celia assured them, "Eliza and I will look after the house. Don't worry, just enjoy your holiday."

The house felt empty without Auntie Nelly and Uncle Chris. I missed Auntie Nelly's cooking. Both Celia and I were so busy and most often we just opted for takeaway food.

One day Celia hinted, "Hey Eliza, your 24th birthday will be coming. Now is the time for celebrations. Invite your friends and I will also invite mine."

At first I was reluctant, but at the end I agreed. "Why not? This is my first birthday party in Australia, let's do it!"

The following weekend Celia and I were busy shopping for the things we need for the party. I asked Celia why we had so much alcohol — spirit, wine, beer and champagne — and she laughed and said, "Eliza, my friends and your friends love to drink and it is your 24th birthday. Let's let our hair down! It will be a party you won't forget. Mum and Dad are away. Let's take the opportunity." I just kept quiet.

The 25th of November was my birthday and fell on a Saturday as a bonus. Celia decorated the house with lots of posters and banners — she'd really gone overboard. She was more excited than me in celebrating my birthday. She organised all the hors d'oeuvres and the main course; with around 25 people invited, it would be a smorgasbord of meat, chicken, seafood and desserts.

Before the arrival of our guests, I hurriedly changed my outfit to a body-hugging red dress with a low cut at the front that showed my nice cleavage. Celia commented, "My gosh Eliza, you are stunningly gorgeous."

I blushed and smiled. "Thanks Celia. Is this too revealing? I can change."

"Oh no! If you got the figure, why not show it?"

The guests started arriving around 6.00 pm, complimenting both of us on how beautifully the house was decorated for the occasion. All of them were raving about the food and the variety of alcohol selections.

All of us had a wonderful time, with karaoke singing, dancing and lots of laughter. I was so happy. Finally

I found my new life, despite past experiences and heart-aches that were now a thing in the past and buried forever.

The last guests left around 11.30 pm. Celia and I were fully exhausted. The whole house was a mess with bottles and glasses everywhere. "What would Auntie Nelly and Uncle Chris say if they were here?"

Celia gently pulled me to her side and advised, "Eliza, don't worry, we will clean the mess tomorrow. You are a little tipsy, you need rest." Celia was right; I was exhausted even though I didn't have a lot to drink. I was little bit lightheaded and uncoordinated. I walked to my room and fell asleep at once.

I woke up around 4.00 am. Celia was on my side, hugging me tightly. Still feeling drowsy I asserted, "Celia, why are you in my room?"

She did not answer my question. Instead she put her fingers into my vagina; I felt her rubbing me gently. I wanted her to stop but enjoyed every minute of it. For the first time I tasted ecstasy, an explosion of emotions, that sent shivers through my whole body. I was breathless; I felt the woman in me. It was an intense, unmeasurable joy and happiness.

Celia asked me to do the same for her. Now I yearned to be inside her. Her lips met mine, kissing me passionately; while caressing my breast and stroking my whole body, she whispered how she fell in love with me the moment she saw me at the airport.

Celia had a firm sculptured body, a pleasure for my fingers to touch. We made love for hours until, exhausted, both of us had fallen asleep. Our bodies entwined, wrapped around each other. It was almost noon when both of us woke up like children. We made love again, virtually for the whole day, only resting to eat.

We cleaned the mess at 8.00 pm, then Celia cooked a quick dinner for the two of us. I told her about my experience of being gang-raped during my last year of university — of the trauma and the nervous breakdown, and how that was the main reason for not wanting to have any relationship with men.

Celia was so sympathetic. "Eliza, I'm so sorry to hear that. Don't worry, you are safe with me. I won't break your heart. I will be loyal and will love you till the last breath of my life and that is my promise to you."

By the way Celia, have you really been a lesbian from the start? Do your parents know about this?"

Celia smiled. "No, my parents don't know — this is why I do not have any boyfriend. I'm more attracted to woman to men, this is who I am!"

"Now I know why you are so caring and kind — at times I wonder the reason for it." We both burst into laughter.

My whole body was aching on Monday morning when I went to work. I was happy and in a very good mood, smiling all the time — my friends at work noticed the difference. All of them wondered what got into me, and I responded, "Nothing really, just happy for having such an awesome birthday party."

Celia had taken leave that day to finish up all the cleaning. I couldn't wait to go home and see Celia.

As I came home after work, I could smell the aroma of my favourite meal (and hers): lamb shank in white wine and almost falling of the bone. The house was immaculately clean.

Happy to see me, Celia gave me a tight hug, kissed me and whispered, "So nice to see you, I missed you."

"So did I," I replied. For me this was really a paradise. I found someone who truly loved and cared for me with passion.

We had a nice meal, watched TV and then we went to bed together. We make love, but this time it was more intense. She was kissing me all over my body as if devouring me with gusto. I felt her lips and tongue touch my privates. I screamed with excitement and joy, nearly passing out.

Each day we become closer. We shared the same interests and passions — especially our love of life, arts and music.

At times I wondered if this was too good to be true. On weekends and occasionally on Friday nights I went out with my office friends. Celia was quite jealous every time I went out with friends. I always assured Celia that she was my only love, and she had nothing to worry about.

Before Christmas, I passed my driver's license test. Now my dream of owning a car became a reality. Celia and I spent Christmas quietly at home. I made a long distance call to my parents; it was so good to know they were still healthy. They were asking when I would visit them. Of course I did not mention my relationship with Celia.

Three months passed so quickly; Celia's parents would be arriving within the next few weeks.

Celia went to the airport one Saturday morning to pick them up. Her parents were happy to be back home. Delighted, Auntie Nelly said with affirmation, "Wow, how immaculately clean the house is! Everything is nice and tidy. You girls did a good job looking after the house."

This night was different from the previous nights. Celia was back in her room and I really missed Celia's hugs, kisses and her warm body. But we had to be careful. This was not an ideal time to tell her parents about our relationship.

It was already four months since Celia's parents arrived. During weekends we went to a motel or hotel for a day, just to make love and feel the warmth of our bodies. Celia's parents did not notice any difference until one night.

It was a Saturday evening. Auntie Nelly said, "Celia, Eliza, we will be going to my best friend's birthday. Both of you can come if you want."

But Celia uttered strongly, "We don't feel like going, Eliza and I will just be staying home and watching a movie."

"Okay, it's your choice, but do not wait for us — we will be arriving late."

At last the whole house was ours. We watched an old film: my favourite, *An Affair to Remember.* Then Celia started disrobing. I babbled, "Stop Celia, we have to go to my room."

But Celia insisted, "It's a bit exciting if we make love here on the lounge room floor."

We turned off the light and just left one lampshade alight, giving us a romantic atmosphere. We were both naked and started making love, her on top of me. I could feel intense pleasure; the floor lounge was hard so I could easily reach my climax, feeling the same passion and warmth as we did the first time.

Suddenly the front door opened and lights were switched on; in shock Celia's parents burst into the room in surprise and disbelief. "Eliza, Celia, what's this?"

We both grabbed our clothes.

"What's going on between you?" Auntie Nelly screamed with anger and disgust. "Eliza, you have the nerve to influence my daughter to this filth? We helped you. Is this the repayment we get from you? We took you in with open arms, and treat you as our own in the family, and what we got is this?"

I started crying and sobbing. I was embarrassed and humiliated; no words came from my mouth. I was speechless.

Celia defended me. "It's not Eliza's fault. I was the one who initiated the whole thing. I was too scared to tell both of you the real me! I'm a lesbian, it's the main reason I don't have intimate relationships with guys. I'm so sorry to disappoint both of you."

Auntie Nelly wept, yelled and protested. "Celia, are you just trying to defend and protect Eliza?"

"No, Mum and Dad," Celia assured them, "it's the truth."

Auntie Nelly cried. Uncle Chris hugged her and with confronting words he whispered to her, "Darling, the truth hurts. I know. But we have to accept her as our only daughter. We should be understanding."

I could see the sadness in both of Celia's parents. I could feel their pain. They were a very nice, loving couple and they were really disappointed to learn the truth about their only daughter's choice of life.

When all the emotions settled down, Uncle Chris explained: "We decided to come home early because your mum had a migraine headache. We didn't expect any of this to happen. Eliza, Celia, we'll discuss this thing tomorrow morning, but while you are in my house, *respect* my house — I don't care what you do outside. But not in my house," Uncle Chris demanded strongly.

I went to my room guilty and angry at myself — but on the positive side, it solved our problem of informing them our relationship.

Love encompasses everything
And does not know its boundaries
It is so strong
It will conquer all
Along its path
It does not care who you are
Regardless of gender
Status or beliefs
It makes a strong man cry
And a weak man strong.

Lorna Ramirez

Chapter 7

Acceptance

It was a beautiful sunshine Sunday morning. I had not risen from my bed. I felt drowsy and heavy-eyed. I got only two hours sleep. Auntie Nelly's words stuck in my mind. I felt guilty for this whole mess.

From my bedroom, I heard Celia and her parents in the kitchen having their breakfast. I dreaded this moment. Sluggishly I changed and joined them for breakfast. It was an eerie atmosphere — we were all quiet. Then Uncle Chris broke the silence and said, "We have to talk Celia, right after you finish your breakfast."

Celia and I cleaned the kitchen and then went to the family room, where Celia's parents were waiting for us. I sat beside Celia. Uncle Chris started the conversation. "So what's your plan, Eliza?" I grasped for words. I don't know what to say. Uncle Chris continued talking. "Your auntie and

I would recommend that you find another place to stay. That would be ideal for all of us. We will give you a month's time to look for a place, thus helping you to settle down."

Thanks Auntie, Uncle. I certainly will do that. I do apologise for everything. It was never my intention to hurt your feelings."

Celia interrupted, "Mum, Dad, if Eliza goes, I will be going with her."

"What! Celia, are you out of your mind?" Auntie Nelly said angrily. "Do you know what you are doing? Have you got any shame? What will my friends think and say about the whole thing?"

"Mum, Dad, you only think of yourselves and what other people will say. How about my feelings, my happiness … these are not important to both of you? Please accept who I am," Celia pleaded.

"Okay, you make your choice Celia. Once you are out of that door, forget about us. I won't have a daughter from now on," Auntie Nelly warned.

"Mum, Dad, forgive me — as much as I love both of you, I have to be with Eliza. I do love her and no one can take that away from me. So sorry that I have to choose this."

"Celia, please don't do that. They are your parents. Don't make the decision to disown them," I cried.

"Eliza, my parents made that decision. They cannot

understand and accept who I am. C'mon, pack your things — we're going."

"But where are we going? We still have to find a place to stay," I said in disbelief.

"Don't worry, Eliza. We will be staying for the meantime with my friend, Jimmy. He's got a house in Ascot Vale."

"Please Celia, as your parents, we only want the best for you. Think it over. You are making a big mistake."

"No Mum, Dad. I made my decision and I'm sure I will be happy with my choice."

We left the house. Auntie Nelly was crying with Uncle Chris holding and comforting her. A very sad scene to witness.

Jimmy's house was in Ascot Vale, not far from Essendon where Celia's parents lived. "Hi Celia, so surprised to see both of you. What brought you here?" Jimmy asked.

"Jimmy, we have no place to stay. We were kicked out by my parents. They were shocked and angry upon learning of my relationship with Eliza."

"That's not a problem. You're welcome to stay here while looking for a place to rent," Jimmy replied.

"Thanks Jimmy. I knew you would be able to help."

Celia and I took a few days leave. We started to look for our own place, shopping for our basic equipment: gadgets for the kitchen, appliances, and furniture for our apartment. Both of us were excited to have our own place to live. This was another chapter of my life and at this stage I was so happy. But my only worry was my family. Would they understand and support me for my choice? However, I was prepared to accept all the consequences of my actions.

Jimmy was helping us in any way he could. Really, he was a good friend and a lovely person. After three weeks, Celia came home from work and excitedly announced, "Eliza, we'll have our own flat. It's in Maribyrnong, a walking distance to Highpoint Shopping Centre. It's a unit, two bedroom, close to all amenities, tram, bus going to the city."

"Wow!" I jumped with joy. Now we could ring up for the deliveries of all the furniture and electrical appliances we'd bought.

The key was handed to us and Jimmy helped us moved to our new place.

"This is it, Eliza — our new home. I finally came out of my shell — I'm so relieved that I won't have to pretend and disguise the real me. Thanks Eliza, for being a part of my life and your life," Celia whispered.

"And thank you for giving back my life. You are the first person other than my family whom I've trusted," I told Celia with tenderness.

"I am not that strong to carry you inside Eliza," joked

Celia. I burst into laughter. As we walked inside Celia whispered into my ear, "Eliza, I love you so much. I do not want to lose you. My world will crumble without you." I responded by hugging Celia tight and kissing her lips tenderly — then Celia pinned me down on the floor.

We made love as passionately as ever. Our two bodies became one, our hearts beating so close to one another and our two souls drifting into eternal bliss, feeling that immeasurable happiness we tasted when we made love for the very first time.

We fell asleep curled together, then I woke up and said, "Celia, we still got lots of things to unpack."

"Okay then," responded Celia.

We were so energised arranging and decorating our place. "I want this place to be perfect, warm and full of love," Celia said.

Everything was back to normal. Both of us were busy working; Celia was often overseas or on work assignments and I worked long hours. I liked to be busy; at least my loneliness and missing Celia would be alleviated.

I was doing really well with my job and my dream of becoming a journalist in an Australian newspaper soon came true when David, my supervisor, called me over one day at the office and said, "Eliza, next year Marie will be on maternity leave. You will take her place. We will train you as an apprentice journalist. Your new position will start next year. I am really impressed with the quality of your work. You deserve this promotion."

"Really, David?" I said with excitement. "Thanks for giving me a chance. This is my dream, to be a reporter in an Australian newspaper."

That night I rang Celia, who was in Europe for a conference. Of course she was delighted and couldn't wait to be back home for a celebration. I also rang Mum and Dad. They too were impressed.

"When will you visit us here in the Philippines?" both my parents asked.

I replied, "Soon. Did I mention to you before that Celia and I moved out from her parents' house?"

"Yes, you did. But why the decision?"

"Celia wants to be independent and she can help me pay for my rent."

"Bring her with you when you visit us here in the Philippines," Mum suggested.

"Of course Mum, I will."

At Christmas 1979, I brought Celia to our Christmas function. At the party, all of them congratulated me for my promotion. David, a happily married middle-aged man, was always praising my ability as a worker. Hence, the main reason for his decision for my promotion.

Martin, one of my work colleagues, said, "Eliza, you are not only gorgeous but also a very smart lady. We all love and admire you in our department." Martin raised his glass and proposed a toast. "To Eliza, the most beautiful girl I have ever known to break my heart (everyone burst into laughter). Eliza, for your promotion and success."

Celia was not happy about the whole thing. Jealous and furious, she kept quiet the whole night. My workmates all met Celia when I had my birthday party last year. We left our function at almost midnight.

As soon as we arrived and entered our bedroom, Celia burst into anger. "I am not happy at all, Eliza." Celia stormed out of the bedroom and shut the door loudly.

I followed her and asked, "Have I done anything wrong for you to be so angry?"

"Why did you not mention that we are not just friends, that we are partners and in a relationship? Are you embarrassed? When will you tell them about us?" questioned Celia.

"I will tell them when the time is right," I explained.

"When is the right time?" Celia angrily asked.

"Celia, I suppose I should be open by now regarding our relationship. Is that why you're in a rage? I apologise, from now on, I will introduce you as my partner. I really do love you, and I don't want to hurt your feelings."

At the end, we forgave each other. We made love and

professed our love for each other — it was tender, but at the same time intense, fervent and lustful. For both of us time stood still. Our ardent love for each other would always be alive; that could never be doubted or questioned.

As soon as I was granted my Australian citizenship in the year 1981, we decided to have a month-long holiday in the Philippines. I rang up Mum and Dad and said I would be spending Christmas and New Year with them. I felt sorry for Celia, as until now her parents hadn't forgiven her and stopped communicating with her. My mum and dad asked on the phone if I had some problems with Celia's parents — they stopped sending Christmas cards.

We booked from December 15 to January 15 for our holiday. We were so excited and looking forward to see my family.

It was very busy at Manila International Airport. Mum, Dad, Jose and Carlo were there to meet us. Mum cried with joy, hugged me tight and said, "So happy to see you, Eliza. We all missed you so much."

"So this is Celia, Chris and Nelly's only daughter. How's your mum and dad, Celia?" Dad asked.

Celia replied, "They are in good health and fine."

"Cannot wait to be home, Mum. I'm really missing all the food, the busy street of Manila, the whole atmosphere and surroundings."

"Both of you will have the time of your lives. Christmas is the busiest time of the year here. All the shops, streets and even trees are decorated with dazzling light," my mum boasted.

"I'm sure I will. It's almost 20 years since I last visited the Philippines," commented Celia.

It was almost noon when we arrived home in Quezon City. I had my bedroom while Celia was in a guest room. Celia did not like the idea of us having a separate room. I convinced her that in the next few days I would be telling my parents about us. Celia agreed.

Mum was busy preparing for our late lunch. She cooked my favourite dish: kare-kare, a beef stewed with vegetables in peanut sauce. She also made fresh lumpia: young bamboo shoots stir fried with minced pork and chopped vegies (thinly sliced cabbage, carrots) and wrapped with homemade wrapper.

We rested for the next day, giving me a chance to catch up with my family. We had a wonderful time going to different scenic places; shopping was chaotic, with lots of people at the mall buying Christmas presents. Both of us went crazy shopping for shoes.

From December 16 to December 24, we had a Filipino tradition of attending the "Simbang Gabi" dawn church service. Masses were held daily as early as 3.00 am to 5.00

am. A few times we went with my family. After the mass, there were lots of street vendors outside the church selling puto (rice cake), bibingka (similar to pancake) and puto bumbong: a ground rice cooked in bamboo using a bamboo steamer, then placed in a banana leaf with butter, sprinkled sugar and grated coconut. This was also a chance to meet with friends and relations. This was one of the many Christmas celebrations that I missed in Australia.

On Christmas Eve, we all attended the midnight mass at 11.00 pm. After the mass, we had the "Noche buena", another Filipino tradition: it is a midnight snack of hot food. We had arroz caldo (rice chicken soup) or pancit (Philippine noodles), hot pandesal (sweet bread), hot chocolate or coffee.

It was only the start of the endless gorging of delicious food. On Christmas Day, we had a big hearty Christmas lunch. We always had the traditional Spanish dish of lechon: a suckling pig slowly roasted in a spit over a coal. We also had glazed ham, morcón (rolled beef with ham, boiled egg, spices inside then stewed in tomato sauce) and of course the popular pancit noodles.

After the hearty lunch, gifts were exchanged. Mum, Dad and my two brothers were all excited opening the gifts I bought them from Australia.

My mum and dad gave me a beautiful pearl necklace

and they gave Celia a stunning handbag made from native product. More laughter and bonding for my family. At night, my real aunties, uncles, extended families and friends came. I received from them lots of gifts and we shared another scrumptious and delicious dinner that night.

With our visitors gone, I was about to enter my room when Celia came and asked, "When will you break the news to your parents regarding our relationship, Eliza?"

I said, "Listen Celia, in about a week we will do it together."

Celia agreed, hugged me tight and kissed me on my lips, not aware that Mum was behind her. With shocking disbelief on what she saw, she exploded in anger, "Eliza, what's the meaning of this?"

I was stunned, caught in an awkward situation, but I managed to answer and asked for understanding. "Mum, do not be upset, this is my choice. We are in a relationship. Please understand, Mum. I am happy now." My mum did not say a word and remained silent. Then I asked, "How can I tell Dad?"

My mum replied, "Do not tell your dad, Eliza. He is very sick. He had been diagnosed with pancreatic cancer stage 4, with only months to live."

"What? Why did you not inform me?" I'd asked him at

the airport if he was okay. He looked so weak and frail but he said he was feeling fine.

"He does not want you to worry," explained Mum. "Be careful with all your actions, Eliza and Celia. Your dad should not know about the whole thing."

The New Year celebration is the noisiest day of the year. Fire crackers in different forms and sizes were used by everyone, even though they are prohibited. Pots and pans were clanged, scaring off evil spirits and bad luck. Trucks and cars blew their horns to greet the coming year.

We all dressed up in polka dots (symbolising money), a Filipino superstition to have a good luck and money coming in for the coming year. Before midnight, the doors and windows were left open to allow good luck to enter. Children jumped as high as they could, believing they would become taller for the following year.

After midnight, we had our "Noche buena" (midnight meal). Special foods were prepared by Mum and the helpers. We had pancit palabok (seafood noodles with ground pork), malagkit (glutinous sticky rice), pandesal (sweet bread), leche flan (crème caramel) and lots of round fruits (such as grapes, oranges, apples). The round shape of the fruits symbolised money or good luck for the coming year. Another one of the many celebrations I missed in Australia. Indeed, I did have the best Christmas and New Year.

As always, happiness and good things came to an end. It is time for us to back to Australia.

I really hated goodbyes; leaving my family for the second time was even harder than the first time. Dad decided not to go to the airport. I respected his decision. Deep within, he knew this would be the last time to see me. It really broke my heart.

My brothers Jose and Carlo were also saddened seeing me go. I hugged both of them, reminding them to look after our parents, especially Dad. Mum hugged me and gave me her blessings, assuring me that whatever decision I made in life, she would support me.

I had taken another few days leave while Celia started work the following day. We were busy as usual. I often worked long hours and Celia went overseas for work related reasons. There were times Celia and I don't see each other for a month or two but we always make up for the lost time we had. Our love for each other grew stronger and stronger.

Acceptance

It's easy to love the lovable
It's easy to accept people
Who share our beliefs and convictions
It's easy to love families and friends
It will take courage for us
To love and accept people
Who are different, unlovable
The world would be a peaceful place
If we tried to accept and respect everyone
Regardless of gender, race or
Religion and other differences

From *My Innermost Thoughts* by Lorna Ramirez

Chapter 8

Shattered Dreams

Eight months after my holiday, I received the sad news that my dad had passed away. "Eliza, you don't have to be back again," advised Mum. But I insisted and said, "Mum, I want to see Dad for the last time. Surely my supervisor would understand my situation."

I took a week of compassionate leave. Celia did not go with me this time. It is the saddest moment, going home to see your dad in a coffin. There were times I couldn't cry anymore. I felt sorry for Mum, but she was a strong person and I was sure she could manage to pull through. My two brothers still lived at home and they would help Mum during her grieving process.

The entombment was very emotional. Lots of friends and extended family attended. Dad was so popular in our community. He was known not only as a businessman but also a philanthropist, very active in charities helping people, especially the destitute and the poor.

In the Philippines, from the day that a person passed away, we prayed and started rosary and novena for nine consecutive days, but the burial would be done within three to four days.

On the ninth and final day of the novena and rosary, lots of people came for mass so a banquet of food was served for those who attended. I did not wait for this and my family understood my situations.

Arriving in Australia was a different feeling this time, as I worried about my mum. I had to stay focused and strong. My life was now in Australia and I was totally committed to my relationship with Celia. I was also positive that my two brothers would be able to look after Mum, especially now that Dad was gone.

Celia and I had a good income, so we decided to take our relationship to the next level and buy a house instead of renting. It was also a good investment and I knew we could easily afford it.

It was quite exciting attending house auctions at weekends. I could feel now that my life with Celia was real and would be forever.

One day Celia said, "Eliza, after we get our new house, the only thing missing in our lives is a baby. We can probably adopt either a relative on your side or overseas."

I replied, "Celia, still too early to think about it."

"It's only a suggestion Eliza," Celia explained.

We finally found a decent house in Williamstown. The house overlooked Hobson Bay. From the house you could see the magnificent Melbourne skyline. It was also walking distance to lots of cafes, pubs and nice restaurants. During weekends, the place was bustling with activities. It was indeed a dream place for us. I could have my early morning jog before I went to work breathing the fresh air coming from the sea. I was so excited to live in this area.

This place was so memorable to both of us. When I first arrived in Australia, Celia took me here. Straight away I fell in love with the place.

It was 1982 when we moved to this beautiful place. I was over the moon. Everything was rosy and perfect for the first time in my life. I felt complete contentment and wondered at times if this was too good to be true.

We had a housewarming party, attended by our friends. Now it was official that Celia and I were in a serious relationship. All of our friends were happy for us.

Quite often I rang up Mum, glad to hear she was coping quite well. I invited Mum to visit us in Australia but she always declined my invitations.

Even after years in our new home, Celia had still gotten no communication from her parents. I could feel the pain. She was hurting inside and at times tried to hide it from me. It was so sad that her parents couldn't understand and support their only daughter.

It was one of those weekends while we were having our breakfast at the café restaurant when Celia said, "Eliza, we've been in our house for almost three years. I think it's about time to have a family by adopting a baby girl. What do you think?"

I quickly replied, "But Celia, both of us are busy, who will look after the baby?"

"Don't worry about that. We can afford to get a nanny. The baby would really add colour and joy to our already blessed life," Celia explained. "As soon as I get back from my overseas trip, we'll talk it over. I will be going to Beijing for about two months and then to Japan for a week before I return to Australia."

The following day I rang up Mum, encouraging her to be in Australia once we were be able to adopt a baby. Mum was so supportive; I was blessed in having a wonderful family.

Five years in my work, I was promoted to become a senior reporter. The new role had lots of responsibilities but I enjoyed the challenges given to me. Each day was different; anything could happen, and the surprises gave me the drive to work harder.

During the two months Celia was away, I started missing her so I buried myself in work, staying late at night. My workmates tried their best to help me. At times, we go out for a drink or two at a bar and during weekends we'd go to nightclubs. Yet my heart ached — I missed Celia.

At last Celia would be coming home. I woke up in a good mood that Saturday morning. It was a glorious day; being summer, the sun shone brightly through my window, warming my face.

I hurriedly made my bed; Celia would be coming home tonight. I'd cook her favourite dish, slow cooked lamb shank, and her favourite dessert, egg caramel. I missed her so much; I couldn't imagine my life without her.

I finished all my chores and cooking at around 4.00 pm, and I bought beautiful red roses, which Celia would love. I put on my nice dress then got ready to meet Celia at the airport. It took me more than an hour to get from Williamstown to the airport.

It was a chaotic scene at the airport. There, I heard a shocking announcement. Flight 123, Japan Airlines took off from Tokyo at 18.12 and 12 minutes later, while ascending at a very high speed, a vibration occurred. Rear pressure had ruptured, causing damage to the rear end of the plane.

The plane started descending and burst into flame. I hadn't watched the news so I missed it!

Relatives were screaming and crying. My whole body felt numb. I passed out, hit my head on the floor and woke up at the hospital.

"Where am I?" I muttered.

"You are in a hospital. You passed out at the airport and hit your head ... but do not worry, it's only a mild concussion. You will be okay," advised the nurse. "Did you have a friend aboard that plane?"

"No, no ... this is not happening. This is just a dream. This is not true." I started to shake and scream, then they gave me an injection to calm me down.

I was still in sedation when my friends at the office visited me.

The following day, my workmate Marie took me home. Marie said, "Eliza, you should take at least two weeks leave to arrange for everything, the wake and the funeral. We are going to help you in whatever way we can. David is extending his deepest sympathy for what happened."

Marie stayed for a few days at my place. I could hardly eat. I felt my heart, body and soul had drifted away from me. I was not myself anymore. Part of me died and there was no reason for me to live without my Celia.

That night, I rang up Mum and delivered the sad

news. Without hesitation Mum said, "Eliza, I will be going to Australia ASAP. I will help you. Please be sensible and don't do anything drastic. This time you have to be strong. Just remember, you still have your family who loves you," she pleaded.

"I will try my best to overcome and pull through," I replied.

Within the next four weeks, Celia's body arrived. I did not expect it would take that much time to identify bodies from the plane. So I needed more leave to arrange the wake and the funeral.

At the wake, Celia's parents came. I confronted them and angrily said, "What are you doing here? You are not supposed to be here. Your daughter's been dead to you for years. There is no sense in both of you coming here."

"But we want to see our only daughter for the last time. Please Eliza, we want to pay our respects to Celia," the parents pleaded, sobbing and crying.

Mum came to my side and said, "Eliza, please forgive them!"

"No Mum, I cannot. They disowned their own daughter and I am sure Celia would say the same thing."

The parents left the wake broken-hearted. They now realised their mistake. I knew I made the right decision.

Ode to the lost loved one
Happiness and life together we once had
Has been taken away from us
All those that we shared, those precious moments
And precious times that we had
It's now just past memories
It's all that I have
They say time will heal the pain I feel
But the scar and loneliness in my heart
Will always be here
That will never take time
To heal

From *My Passion, My Calling* by Lorna Ramirez

Chapter 9

Heartaches and Miseries

I struggled to cope with the loss of my beloved Celia. Mum decided to stay for another three months — and that would help me a lot. I requested another two months leave. My superior agreed and understood my situation.

My workmates Sue, Tina, and Marie were always visiting, giving me comforting words. Tina then asked, "Have you been eating properly and sleeping well, Eliza? You seem to have lost a lot of weight."

Marie agreed, "Yes, you cannot go on like this. You are still young and smart and pretty. You have a bright future ahead of you."

I started sobbing and said, "I cannot bear this anymore. I'm so lonely and terribly missing Celia."

"Listen Eliza, no one can help you but yourself. Be

strong. If you cannot do it yourself, you have to seek professional help," suggested Sue.

"No Sue," I argued, "I do not want to have the stigma of going to a psychiatrist. I'll try my best to do it on my own. I'm pretty sure I'll be able to handle this."

My nightmares came back; I would scream in my sleep, and Mum would come rushing to my side. Often she stayed by my side all through the night.

One Saturday morning, Mum went to do our groceries. I was alone in our house. Feeling very lonely at that time, I took sleeping pills, swallowing a lot of them. I started having blurred vision — then I felt dizzy and passed out.

I found myself at the hospital again. Nurses and doctors were trying to pump out the contents of my stomach, using salt water to get rid of the tablets. I was made to vomit, to spit out what pills I could. A charcoal neutraliser countered the effect of the pills. Antiemetic drugs were also given to me to relieve nausea.

By the time they transferred me to a room, I was fully conscious. In the room, my mum and officemates Sue, Marie, Tina and Martin were all waiting for me. I cried when I saw them and with an agonising tone, I said, "So sorry Mum, to give you this problem. I'm so lonely and really missing Celia."

Mum replied with a loving tone, "Eliza, remember you

still have your family and friends, who love and care for you. We will be devastated if something happens to you. Please, promise you won't do this again!"

Hugging Mum, I assured her that this wouldn't happen again. I really felt sorry for her and I regretted what I had done.

Because of my fragile mental state, the hospital transferred me to an inpatient hospital psychiatric ward. I resisted at first but the doctor explained, "This is a good choice for the treatment for your depression."

The inpatient wards had a more residential, casual feel and atmosphere. It was more like a dormitory, with single, shared or double rooms. I was given a single room. At the ward, there was a community room with chairs, sofas, a TV, recreational activities like painting and a piano, and phones so we could get in contact with loved ones and friends. However, the hospital zone was locked up and rules for visitation time, permissible clothing and jewellery needed to be followed.

My medication was monitored very closely. Talk Therapy was twice a week, usually in a group and sometimes on a one to one basis.

In one of the group meetings I attended, they invited a popular psychiatrist, Dr Tony McLaren, to mediate. He was a tall, good-looking guy, quite young, probably five years older than me. He listened attentively to all our problems, being very supportive and giving several suggestions to help members of the group identify their underlying problems.

I was very impressed with the way he conducted our group therapy. He specialised in depression and trauma.

At the end of the session, I was reluctant to approach him but at the end, I shyly asked, "Dr McLaren, my name is Eliza Martinez. Would you be able to help me once I will be released?"

I would never forget the way he smiled and said, "Of course, Eliza, I will help you. Here is my card, you can call me anytime."

I was elated; I knew I could trust him. He was a very good psychiatrist. But at the back of my mind, I was still determined to pull through and overcome my depression without any clinical help.

The ward was not a permanent residence for patients, so at the end of my second week's stay at the hospital I would be released. The hospital strongly suggested continuous care in their partial hospital program. Doctors assured that in this kind of program and treatment, I would be able to go on with my daily chores, or even go back to work. In the meantime, I still had to take my medication and attend group therapy at the hospital.

On a beautiful Saturday in spring, I cheerfully packed

my things, so excited to go home. Marie and Mum picked me up and we drove home.

As I entered the house, a big *surprise!* My officemates and Celia's friends were all there, giving me a very warm welcome. They decorated the house with a big poster: 'Welcome home Eliza. We all love and care for you.'

I was deeply touched and overwhelmed. I hugged my mum and cried with happiness, realising lots of people did care for and love me.

They stayed at my place all afternoon. Marie and Tina were the last ones to go, helping Mum clean up the mess. They did not want me to help. I was pretty tired so I rested. Tina and Marie left our house at almost 7.00 pm. Before leaving, both of them hugged me and said, "Eliza, if you need anything, do not hesitate to call. We will be here at your beck and call."

I replied, "Thanks guys, so lucky to have you as my friends!"

I slept well that night. Mum had hidden my sleeping pills, only giving me any if it was absolutely necessary. She said, "It's just a precaution."

My medication was continuous and I kept to it religiously. I was also attending a few group therapies at the hospital.

In spite of all these treatments and therapies, it seemed

futile. My nightmares continued. Every now and then, I took sleeping pills, crying a lot for no reason, thus making Mum deeply concerned. Slowly going downhill, my appetite and sleep were affected and I started losing weight.

I rang my superior and requested an indefinite leave. He said I could be back whenever I was ready. They hired a temporary replacement while I was on leave.

With things getting out of hand, on Friday morning I rang up Dr McLaren. My heart beat so fast; I didn't know whether I was making the right decision. Luckily he was at his office that day. I introduced myself, but he said, "Yes, Eliza, I do remember you. So you finally decided to see me and seek help."

I choked at first, lost for words. I did not know what to say but after regaining my composure, I answered shyly, "Yes, I want to seek help and I'm positive you would be able to help me."

"Of course I can," assured the doctor. "I will do everything to get you back to your normal life."

"Thank you Dr McLaren," I replied.

He continued, "Your first session will be on Saturday next week in the morning, around 10.00 am. My office is on Collins Street in the city — my address is on the card I gave you. Be sure to bring someone with you on your first session."

"I will, Doc."

"See you then. Looking forward to seeing you for our first session, Eliza," he said.

I hang up the phone, relieved that I had the courage to seek medical help. I was so tired of my rollercoaster of emotions. My friends were right: I had to do something about my problem. I had to seek medical help.

There are times we want to leave
Away from our past
But our past never leaves us
Keeps on haunting us
Wherever and whenever we are
And it is up to us to accept
And deal with it courageously.

From *My Passion My Calling* by Lorna Ramirez

Chapter 10

Psychotherapy

I was curled up in my bed, hugging a pillow, when I heard a knock on my door.

"Eliza, what's wrong? You skipped your breakfast."

"Please come in, Mum."

With a worried look on her face, Mum said, "Are you okay?"

"I'm okay. Nothing to worry about."

Then Mum continued, "I cooked your favourite dish. Please prepare yourself so we can have lunch together."

Celia and I loved the slow-cooked lamb. I showed Mum how to do it when I visited her in the Philippines. Now she could cook it very well.

At the table, I was quiet and did not say a word. Mum anxiously asked, "Is there something bothering you, Eliza?"

Reluctantly I answered, "Mum, I'm not quite sure if I

made the right decision. I rang up Dr McLaren, a psychiatrist I met at the hospital. I will be seeing him next Saturday."

Beaming, Mum said, "Of course, Eliza, without a doubt you made the right decision. At last my prayers had been answered. I know it takes a lot of courage from you to seek help, and this is the best thing you've done."

"Mum, in my first visit, the doctor suggested I should bring along someone with me."

Without hesitation, Mum said, "I would love to come."

The night prior to my first appointment, I couldn't sleep. I keep on tossing and turning, dealing with mixed emotions of fear, uncertainty and hope.

Mum and I arrived 20 minutes early at the clinic. I was so impressed with what I saw in the nice, cosy waiting room. The receptionist, smiling, told us to have a seat, and offered us a cup of tea or coffee. We politely declined. "Dr McLaren will be here shortly," assured the receptionist.

Five minutes later, Dr McLaren arrived, the same infectious smile on his face as the first time I saw him at the hospital. He greeted us with enthusiasm.

After a few minutes, the receptionist said, "Dr McLaren is now ready to see you, Miss Martinez."

We went inside the consulting room, and I was impressed. A beautiful fireplace, a big nice swivel chair and beside it a long, comfy couch. At the far end of the room, there was an antique wood table with two handcrafted wooden chairs.

"Hello Eliza. So glad to see you again. Good of you to bring someone with you."

"Dr McLaren, this is my mum."

"Pleased to see you, Mrs Martinez. Please, both of you, have a seat as I will discuss and explain what to expect about the ongoing therapy."

"Thanks, Dr McLaren."

"You can call me Tony. I'm comfortable with that." Tony continued, "Eliza, you will have twice a week therapy sessions for the next few months. And if I can see progress, I will make it once a week. Mrs Martinez, Eliza needs your support and understanding. Eliza, I will give you antidepressant medication — rest assured it's unlike Valium. This is not addictive if given at the right dose. You won't crave it once you stop taking it. And Mrs Martinez, you are doing a great job supporting Eliza."

"By the way, Dr McLaren ... I mean, Tony. My mum's visa will soon expire. In my fragile condition, I need someone to be with me. Can you possibly help us by writing to the embassy to justify the extension of my mum's visa for at least a year, or until I'm back on my feet?"

"I do understand, and I'll help your mum get the

extended visa for until you've completely overcome your mental illness," Tony promised to both of us.

"Thanks Tony, I really appreciate that."

Then Tony said to my mum, "Mrs Martinez, the first interview will last for 45 minutes, if you can please wait outside. I think Eliza can be on her own for the rest of her therapies."

As Mum left the room I sat on the comfortable, long couch and Tony said, "You can lie down if you like and make yourself feel at home." The couch was at the left side, where Tony sat. His chair was arranged at an angle, not facing me directly. He made sure I was relaxed and explained the purpose and the process of the therapy. "I will be writing notes and I will take down relevant issues. I promise everything will be confidential. These will help me assess your situation."

"It's okay Tony, I can deal with that. Since you will be doing twice a week therapy, I want each session to be informal as possible."

Tony continued by asking the first question: "Tell me about your problems."

I choked again. I couldn't find the words to answer. I was trembling and my tears started flowing.

"It's alright, Eliza. Breathe deeply. Remember, I'm your friend. I'm here to help. Close your eyes. Think and compose yourself. Now once you're ready, please tell me everything I should know."

After five minutes of silence: "I'm ready."

"That's good. I will be listening and as I said before, everything will be confidential."

I started talking and he let me speak freely without interruptions.

The highlight of my session was the loss of Celia — and how her parents treated her and disowned her as their daughter. We also discussed the loss of my father and how much I missed my brothers, relatives and friends in the Philippines.

"Well done Eliza. Good work. Is there anything else I should know?"

I smiled and said, "That's it. Tony, I cannot cope without Celia. She is my world. I really find it difficult to keep on living without her."

"That's why you're here," commented Tony. "At least we made some progress. That will be enough for today. By the way, what preferred days would you like to come?"

"I think I will be doing Saturdays and Wednesdays," I suggested. "Is that okay?"

"Sure," he said. "Let's make it 9.30 am."

When I left the doctor's room, Mum asked, "How did it go?"

"It's okay. I promise to you, this time I will make sure it will work."

"That's my girl," Mum proudly said.

True to his promise, Tony had written to the Australian Embassy. In less than a month, we received a compassionate letter from the embassy approving my mum's extended visa. We were so elated.

After six months, I was still going to my therapy sessions. I felt I was getting better, with a marked improvement in my outlook in life. I learned to trust Tony and at times I wondered if I'd started to like him or if it was just one of those doctor-patient relationships where mutual trust, respect and knowledge developed.

One sunny Saturday morning, I woke up in a good mood, preparing myself to see Tony. On time with my appointment as always, Tony greeted me with a smile. I made myself comfortable and we discussed our previous session. This session was my most memorable.

Tony begin to ask about my sexuality. "Eliza, now that I've earned your trust, I want to know the real you. During your younger days, were you already attracted to the same sex? When did you realise you were different from other girls your age?"

I was astonished that this question came up. I grasped

for an answer. I started crying and sobbing. Then Tony said, "Eliza, I have to know your past, your inner self. Please understand I can do more to help you if you tell me everything. I really want you to get back your life."

"Yes, I know. I keep on running from my past and at times I feel helpless. Then I came to know Celia — she was the one who gave me life, love and hope. And for a while, I had forgotten my past. Listen, no one knows what happened to me except our family doctor and Celia. I was gang-raped by four young, influential, wealthy men way back in my university days." Again, I started sobbing and crying. But I had the courage to describe my ordeal in detail to Tony. Because of this dark moment in my life, I was scared of having a romantic relationship with the opposite sex. I'd started to hate all men. I was scarred for life.

"I migrated to Australia to forget my past. Celia came into my life and brought back the laughter, happiness and joy that I have never felt for years. Now she is gone, so is my life. Wow!" I added, "Come to realise it, now I'm telling all these to you, Tony. You are the first man I've trusted and that is scary."

Tony laughed and said, "I'm your psychiatrist and I'm here to help you. Trust me Eliza, we can do this with your help."

"Thanks Tony, getting everything off my chest is a

great relief for me. I feel I'm not a prisoner of my past. I feel free!"

I was getting better. He was such a good doctor, very thorough and focused in his investigation and assessment. Slowly but surely, I was getting there.

In one of my sessions, he mentioned that his job was done for me and my last session would be the following week. He said, "I will refer you to a very good psychiatrist. You are doing great, Eliza. You are on the mend. Listen, my wife and I will be going to the US for a year. I will be doing a one-year scholarship. My suggestion is you can go back to work — that will keep you busy and speed up your recovery. Please continue the session once a week with Doctor Smith. I know you will be in good hands."

I had mixed emotions for my last session with Tony; I was happy for his success but sad I wouldn't be seeing him anymore. At the end of the session he gave me a friendly hug. I felt a different feeling at that moment when his arms were wrapped around me. A feeling of surrender, trust and most especially bliss that I hadn't felt since Celia.

This week was exactly one year of absence from work. I went to the office that day. They were all surprised and happy to see me. My manager David said, "Eliza, like I said on the phone yesterday, you are most welcome to be back at work."

I replied, "That is so nice to hear that, David. And yes, I'm ready to be back."

"When can you start?" David asked.

I commented, "Soon. Possibly Monday week. I'm ecstatic that I still have a position in the company ... and really happy to feel welcome in spite of my long absence."

At times we cry within
Yet no one can hear
The pain and hurt only you can feel
Those shattered dreams and memories of yesteryears
That haunt you vividly as they can
Years have passed and things have changed
Once again triumphantly you emerge now
A better stronger person

From *My Innermost Thoughts* by Lorna Ramirez

Chapter 11

Entanglement

It was almost six months since Dr McLaren had referred me to another psychiatrist, Dr Smith. A man in his sixties, he was supportive, pleasant and very thorough. I only saw him once a week. I felt I was ready to face the world again, especially at work, and I felt the warm welcome from my workmates. I couldn't wait to be back and start over again.

At the dinner table, my mum said, "Eliza dear, I think you are on the mend. Can I possibly leave you and be back home? I'm missing your brothers and my friends."

"It's okay Mum, I can look after myself."

"Thanks Eliza, but I will wait for a month or so until you are settled in your job."

I appreciated her support.

Tuesday was the D-Day: my first day at work. Mum

rose early and prepared my breakfast. I woke up with full anticipation, but at the same time I was dubious if I was ready to be back.

At the office David started briefing me on my work and explained, "Eliza, you've been away for over a year and to make things easier for you, be my assistant coordinator, organising all the sensitive issues being dealt within the department. I'm sure you can handle it with flying colours," assured David.

"Thanks, I will give my best shot."

After work, my workmates decided to go out as a welcome bash celebration for my first day back at work. We went to this bar in Elizabeth Street called Workshop, one of our favourite hangouts. On a Tuesday night, they had live acoustic experimentation and several talented musicians showcasing their talents. They had a nice selection of cocktails and wines, and the food wasn't bad at all and affordable. I felt happy to be once again in the group. Tina then proposed, "Let's celebrate for Eliza's return!" We all laughed.

It was almost midnight when I arrived home. Mum was still awake and waiting for me. "Mum, you're still awake!" I'd rang to tell her I would be late.

"Yes I know," Mum answered. "I just can't sleep."

"Oh Mum, I'm okay. I can take care of myself." I gave my mum a hug and a kiss.

My progress was really going well. I was so happy to be with all my friends at work, helping me forget the trauma I had experienced. After a few months, David suggested I could return to my previous position as a supervisor in our department. Mum had gone back to the Philippines. She was confident that I could manage on my own. I buried myself in work, ignoring would-be suitors. Dr Smith was happy to release me, giving me a positive evaluation.

Even if Christmas was still three months away, I started doing my Christmas shopping. Summer would arrive soon and I dreaded the hot weather in Melbourne.

Days and months were gone so fast; it was almost a year since I was diagnosed with depression. I wondered where Dr McLaren was. Still in America? He said it would take a year for his wife's contract to finish.

One Friday afternoon, I decided to do my shopping in the city at Myer. The store was packed with shoppers. I bought lots of perfumery, for myself and for presents. I was in a hurry as I had to attend Sue's party. Then I heard a familiar voice: "Miss, miss! You forgot one of your bought items."

I turned around. "Mr McLaren!" I said with amazement. "What are you doing in Melbourne? I thought you were still in America! How is your wife? Is she with you?"

With a thrill in his voice Tony replied, "I have to be in

Melbourne to attend to some business matter. My wife is still in America. You are looking well, Eliza."

I blushed and shyly said, "You are also looking well as always, Mr McLaren."

"Oh c'mon Eliza, call me Tony. Would you mind having a cup of coffee with me? I do love to catch up with you. Tell me about everything — and of course, your progress."

Without hesitation I said yes. He took me to Brunetti Café, an upmarket café then at Melbourne City Square. My heart was beating fast — that smile was really infectious and melted my heart. He listened with enthusiasm about my progress and was happy upon learning I'd gone back to work. "I'm impressed with your recovery, Eliza. That's the way to go. You should be responsible for your own actions. Very proud of you." For the first time I could relate to and feel comfortable with the opposite sex.

That meeting was followed by several dinners. It made me feel guilty, having an affair with a married man. My workmates noticed the big change in me. I was always so happy and cheerful that Sue asked me one day, "Eliza, what has gotten into you? You've changed a lot in the last few weeks. Have you met someone who stole your heart?"

I just smiled and ignored the question. This was a complete turnaround of my life. I felt fully alive but at times scared — Tony was a married man and I was the woman between them.

When I confessed my guilt to Tony, he consoled me and said, "Listen, for the last few months our marriage was already on the rocks. We've grown apart to a point where I cannot talk to her sensibly anymore, so don't feel guilty. Within a month I will be back in America and before I leave, I want to take you to my holiday house in Merimbula. Have you been there?"

"No, I've been to Sydney but not Merimbula."

"Good," Tony said. "We will be driving, stopping over at Lakes Entrance for two days before heading to Merimbula. We'll be staying at our holiday house for a week, then we'll drive along the Snowy Mountains to Canberra. It's a breathtaking view up there. From Canberra we'll drive to Gundagai, staying overnight. Then heading back to Melbourne."

"Wow, you've already worked it out." Feeling hesitant about Tony's preposition I answered, "I'll think about it. I'm not sure if I can continue seeing you."

"Okay, I respect that. I will call you in three days for your answer — and by the way, in case you will go you need two weeks leave."

I couldn't sleep that night. I kept on asking myself, was I ready for a serious relationship? But without a doubt I was madly in love with him. He was the first person other than Celia who gave me back my life.

At the office, I was still contemplating whether I would go with Tony — I didn't even notice Sue asking me questions about work. "What's the matter, Eliza? Is there any problem?"

"No it's okay," I said defensively.

After three days Tony rang — and I couldn't believe I said yes!

"That's my girl, I know you will be enjoying this trip."

The following day, I filed two weeks leave starting the 2nd week of March. It would be autumn — a milder time to travel. "Where are you going?" David asked.

"To Merimbula in NSW."

"That's a very nice tourist spot. Enjoy your holiday."

While I was packing my things, in my mind I was so scared to be with Tony on this trip. I had never been intimate with the opposite sex, and I wasn't sure how I would handle this kind of situation. I packed some revealing lingerie that I'd purchased the other day, not believing that I was doing this.

Tony picked me up early Saturday at 8.00 am. He was in a good mood. "C'mon Eliza, it will take us four hours' drive to Lakes Entrance. We're booked for two nights at the Waverley House Cottage. It's a stunning private place only 2.5 kilometres from the city centre. For sure this trip will be the best time in your life."

It was a comfortable 20°C, pleasant for driving. I was impressed with the place. It was a very peaceful and beautiful landscape — there were also solar heated pools, a Jacuzzi and a gazebo. An ideal romantic escape.

Exhausted from driving, Tony and I rested, had a quick lunch and then explored the area. Lakes Entrance is approximately 320 km from Melbourne. It is almost at sea level, surrounded by various lookouts.

At night we went to the Floating Dragon Chinese restaurant. Heading back to the cottage afterwards, I started to get cold feet. I wasn't ready to be intimate with Tony.

"What's wrong?" Tony asked, "You're very quiet. Are you not enjoying your trip?"

"It's nothing, Tony. I'm just scared. I'm not ready for this."

"Don't worry, I understand. I can wait." True to his promise Tony slept at the other room.

I woke up afresh again, after a good night sleep. Then I heard Tony knock. "We will be busy today, Eliza. We'll be going to Buchan Cave, a popular tourist spot in the area, so we must leave soon after breakfast."

I was enthralled and dazzled by the beauty of the cave, the wonder of nature. The cave was well lit; it had a walkway and a constant temperature of 17°C (63°F) all year round. It took us 45 minutes from Lakes Entrance to Buchan Cave. We went to a nearby café afterwards with all homemade food. I was so happy I decided to go on this trip.

We are back at the cottage late in the afternoon. We didn't feel like going out that night so we just had take-away. Tony opened a bottle of red. We consumed it all and I started to feel a little bit tipsy. Tony hugged me lightly. I wasn't put off by his actions; instead I whispered in Tony's ear, "I'm yours tonight."

Bewildered, Tony said, "Are you sure? I can wait. I don't want to pressure you on doing this."

"Of course, I'm ready," I replied laughing. "Wait, first I have to change to something special."

When I came out of the room with the red revealing lingerie, Tony's his jaw dropped. "Gosh Eliza, you look really gorgeous ... and sexy." He pulled me down the bed and whispered, "You don't need this lingerie, I will strip you naked."

In return I said, "I will also strip *you* naked."

He kissed me, starting from my toe up to the sensitive part of my body. It pushed my sexual excitement to the maximum. I nearly passed out with pleasure. Then he moved up, caressing my breast with his tongue, finally reaching my mouth. Such a passionate moment of love, lust and ecstasy. After savouring my body, he began the rhythmic motion, in and out of me, till both of us attained the beautiful, intense climax of joy and happiness from the love we felt with one another. We did this over and over again till both of us were exhausted and fell asleep.

This was the first time I found happiness with the opposite sex. We woke up to the sound of the alarm clock and hurriedly prepared for our checkout at 10.00 am. We started driving to Merimbula, three hours' drive from Lakes Entrance.

Feeling happiness, exuberance and bliss, Tony said, "Eliza, you are glowing with joy. At last you've conquered your fear. You were great last night, forgetting your difficulty in having sexual intimacy with the opposite sex."

"I do agree, you are the first man in my life I've trusted. I do hope you won't hurt my feelings, Tony."

"Of course, I would never do that. I was really attracted since I first laid eyes on you. Anyway," Tony continued. "We're almost there. Merimbula is a beautiful town. We have a holiday unit there. The town's a haven for tourists and holiday-makers, they call it 'The Jewel of the Sapphire Coast'. It's got the best seafood in Australia. Lots of oyster farming in this town. Our holiday unit is within the city centre. I love fishing there and we can still find beautiful deserted beaches."

By the early afternoon we arrived at Tony's unit, a decent sized two bedroom unit with a nice kitchen, and only five minutes to Tura Beach. Wasting no time, we visited the oyster farm, bought two dozen, then went to the grocery to buy some basic food items. "Eliza," Tony warned, "we don't have to cook. We can go to the restaurants."

I replied, "I enjoy cooking at times. I don't feel like eating at the restaurant."

"Okay, okay, just reminding you. Please yourself."

Tony and I started shucking the oysters. He taught me how to do it, but I was hopeless so he ended up doing it all. Slurping these oysters from the shell was fun. So sweet, tasty and fresh. Tony said with a laugh, "Eliza, do you know that oysters is an aphrodisiac? We will be having a sex marathon tonight."

"You dirty man." We both burst into laughter. The love we felt for one another was a stronger aphrodisiac than these oysters.

We did a lot of activities during our stay in Merimbula. We visited Magic Mountain and the Eden Killer Whale Museum. We enjoyed a tasty lunch at the wharf and aquarium, and whale watching during the early morning. We walked leisurely along the boardwalk, enjoying the fresh and clean air. At our last day in Merimbula we went to Tura

Beach. Walking along the seaside, when we felt hungry we went to a casual waterfront café. They had an excellent seafood menu: succulent oysters (again), fresh fish and juicy prawns.

"We will be leaving early tomorrow, Eliza. Did you enjoy your stay here?"

"Of course I did."

"Well, as we drive through the Snowy Mountains for sure you will admire the breathtaking views."

The Snowy Mountains Highway connected New South Wales to the Monaro region. As we went up the view was so breathtaking, with amazing valleys and mountain peaks. It was a steep and winding road, heading up to the range of about 8–36 feet above sea level. There were times I got scared and my heart seemed to stop beating. When we reached to the top of the mountain, Tony said, "Don't worry, you're safe with me. I'm an excellent and efficient driver. I've been here several times."

"Of course. I'm with you — how can I be scared?"

I was so relieved when we started driving on a flat road going to Cooma. It took us three hours to reach Canberra. We toured the Parliament House and the National Museum of Australia.

After a few hours, it was back on the road again. It would take us another two hours to reach the island of

Gundagai, where we would be staying for a night. It was almost five in the afternoon when we saw the Dog on the Tucker Box, a historical monument and tourist attraction. Tony was so tired from driving when we reached Gundagai that we opted to stay in and just dial for takeaway food.

"I can't believe it's all over," I said. "I really enjoyed our trip, especially our stay at Merimbula. Thanks a lot Tony."

"My pleasure," Tony boasted.

After we checked out, Tony asked, "Would you like to stay one night at Albury or go straight to Melbourne?"

"We can just stop at Albury for a quick rest and snack," I suggested to Tony.

"Okay, you're the boss."

"Tony, you can stay at my place if you want — I still have another three days before I go back to work."

Tony agreed for my proposal. We ordered pizza at my place that night and watched TV. I was so exhausted I fell asleep in Tony's arms. Waking up late the following morning, I could smell bacon, eggs and toast. With that infectious smile on his face, Tony said, "Princess, your breakfast is ready," and he laughed.

"Tony, when will you be back in America?"

"In about two months' time, and staying for another three months. Then both my wife Linda and I will be back in Melbourne."

"How about us?"

"What about it? Listen, just give me time as I always say. I do adore and love you so much, just give me time," Tony pleaded.

"I will wait."

Going back to work was even harder after that wonderful, memorable holiday with Tony. At the office, my workmates were asking as a tease if I went with someone special. "When will we meet this person?"

I said, "Soon!"

They all laughed, then Sue said, "At last, the reluctant and elusive heart of Eliza Martinez is conquered. This someone must be really special!" They laughed again.

Tony and I saw each other almost every week, taking advantage of these special moments before he took off to America. Tony was busy with his newly acquired business partnership. In spite of all this we still made time to be with each other. In Tony's arms I felt complete tranquillity; no one mattered to me except him. The night before he left, we booked a room in a five star hotel. We had dinner, listened to the band playing, and went up our room at almost 11.00 pm. Again we consummated our love for each other, as if the world would end tomorrow, as passionate and intense as ever. Fully exhausted, we fell asleep wrapped around each other.

I hated goodbyes. I drove Tony to the airport and he assured me nothing would change — we would be together forever soon.

I buried myself working, to get Tony out of my mind. Martin asked, "What's the matter, having any problems?"

"No, not at all. I just want to be busy." We were so busy at work covering a murder story and everybody was involved. The pressure of my work helped me to adjust this situation.

Tony and Linda would be returning next week. I was so excited to see Tony. I did not ring him for the first few weeks. One afternoon, he rang my office; I was thrilled to hear his voice again. He booked one night at the Hyatt Hotel in Collins Street.

My heart was beating so fast as he greeted me outside my work. As always he looked so handsome and gorgeous. He gave me a kiss and a tight hug. "Tony, I have to go home first, change and bring some things for our overnight stay."

"That's okay," Tony agreed.

We had a mouth-watering dinner: delicious fresh seafood, my favourite juicy tender steak, and desserts to die for. "Hey Tony, are you trying to fatten me?"

He laughed and said, "That would not change a thing, I will still love you regardless."

I blushed. "I love you too. Does your wife know about us?"

"At this stage, no."

"But we've been seeing each other for quite some time. What is our future?" I asked with concern.

Tony quickly said, "Let's not ruin the night. We have to celebrate and truly enjoy the moments we are together."

I kept quiet and Tony tried to cheer me up. Of course the sex was intense, but I felt insecure. I had to be sure that he loved me not only for sex. For the last two years, we had our secret meetings — I loved the escapades, but I was beginning to get sick of the whole thing, doing it over and over again.

On one of our love escapades, staying along the beautiful Great Ocean Road for two nights, I decided to give Tony an ultimatum.

A few times along the way, we stopped for beautiful views and lookouts. We booked a motel in Lorne along the beach, in the heart of the town. Celia and I used to come here. Now I was with Tony; the vacuum left by Celia in my heart had been filled up with him. I wished this would never end.

In the morning, we strolled along the beaches of Lorne, a popular town popular with tourists, on coast and along the Erskine River.

We visited the Erskine Falls; though the rocks were slippery, it offered a picturesque view of the stunning waterfall. I'd been here quite a few times with Celia, but the beauty still amazed me. The Twelve Apostles was one of my favourite sites. In the morning a nice walk along the beach was something to look forward to. The calmness of the sea, while enjoying fresh air with the person you love beside you, is something to be cherished.

As we walked along the beach I said to Tony, "I cannot wait anymore — you have to decide now. It's me or your wife. I had been waiting for more than two years and you always keep on saying, 'Give me time'. Now is the time, Tony."

Tony did not say a word at first, then he broke his silence. "You are right Eliza, next week ... Sunday. I will tell you our future."

"Really? I'm so happy for that. I'm sure you will deliver the good news."

Tony hugged and kissed me tenderly, whispering, "I do not know how I could live without you, Eliza."

The following day we went back to Melbourne, but this time I felt different. I was positive Tony would choose me over his wife, especially now that I was six weeks pregnant with his child. I wouldn't tell him yet; it would be a surprise next weekend. I couldn't wait for that day to come.

A Song of Love

I cannot count the number
of the stars in the sky
But I can see its brightness,
beauty and grandeur
I cannot fathom the depth
of the deep blue sea
But I can see its serenity,
calmness and tranquillity
It's the same
I cannot tell you how much
I love you
It's immeasurable and unending
But I do know and I feel within
my heart, the intensity
of my love for you

Lorna Ramirez

Chapter 12

End of Reminiscing

From the sofa, Eliza looks at the time. *Oh my gosh, she thinks, it's almost 7.30, Tony will be here soon — I'm so carried away reminiscing my past. This will be the most exciting and memorable chapter of my life. Tony and I will forever be together. The pot roast will be cooked to perfection, served with a balanced fruity wine that goes well with the food. The table is all set for the two of us and there's romantic candlelight. An evening of celebration.*

The doorbell rings; Eliza's heart beats fast as she opens the door. "There you are, looking so handsome as always. Come in ..."

"Wait, I want to kiss and hug you first — you are as beautiful as these flowers, Eliza."

"Thanks Tony."

"Always a pleasure, but I will have to tell you something important."

"I do not want to hear that yet, I also have a surprise for you — but first, we have to savour my delicious pot roast with all the trimmings. Then we can discuss everything."

"Wow, this is a perfect pot roast Eliza, cooked so tender and juicy, and really tasty."

"Of course Tony, cooking it with so much love from my heart for this very special occasion. By the way, I made your favourite dessert, leche flan."

"I'll play our favourite song while we have dinner."

"Good idea."

After they eat, Tony says, "For that heavenly dinner, you deserve a hug. I will give you a loving hug — I'll kiss you passionately for the last time!"

"Why Tony, what do you mean by that?"

"Don't worry Eliza, forget what I said ... let's just enjoy this moment of bliss and joy, as if tomorrow will never come."

"Oh Tony, you always make me feel so special ... I'm a complete woman in your arms, and nothing matters when I'm with you."

Both of them make love, intensely and passionately, till they're exhausted.

"So Tony, tell me about your decision, I cannot wait for the news that you'll be leaving your wife so we can always be together. You said I'll know tonight if our relationship will go to the next level ... what's wrong? Tony, your face has gone white."

"Eliza, you know how much I love you ..."

"I know that, all I want you to tell me now is, will you be leaving your wife for me? I want to know your decision."

Eliza ... I'm so sorry to break the news. I cannot leave my wife. She needs me now more than ever."

Silence between both of them.

"What about me, Tony? I need you desperately, can you understand that?" Eliza starts sobbing. "Once you said you would never break my heart — I've been waiting for this moment when we could be with each other forever. Have I done something wrong? I had so many heartaches and miseries, my struggle to be back on my feet after everything I've been through and now this is happening? I don't know how I can go on with my life without you. Did you use me as one of your experiments? You bastard, Tony. You let me fall in love with you, then after years of an intense relationship, dropping me like this ... I hate you!" Eliza is almost hysterical. "You even have the guts to make love to me as if I'm just food to satisfy your palate for the last time! I hate you, I do not want to see you ever again. I do not want to be your mistress, for you to only use for your convenience."

"Don't even think that, our affair was the most beautiful time of my life. Eliza, you will always be a part of my heart, mind and soul. I cannot explain to you the reason for this decision, it's killing me inside, but I know it's for the best."

"I do not want to see you again, Tony." Tony is trying to hug Eliza, but Eliza pushes him away. "Don't, Tony, don't touch me ever again."

"But what about the news you were going to tell me?"

"It's not relevant anymore, it's not important."

"Goodbye Eliza, I will continue loving you for the rest of my life."

I won't give in and be defeated. I will be strong, and raise this child that I am carrying by myself. He does not deserve to know.

Eliza goes to bed, crying all night. The next morning she calls work. "David, I don't feel well, I will be having a day off today."

"It's okay Eliza, not a problem."

"Eliza, are you coming with us tonight for a quick drink?"

"No Sue, I have to finish my report and do a lot of research for our next project."

"Okay, take it easy Eliza. Just wondering ... for the last few weeks you seem to be burying yourself with work, is there something we should know?"

"Oh no Sue, I just want to be busy and finish all my work."

"David, will you be able to help me to transfer to Sydney for the recent position they advertised?"

"Why? Are you not happy working with us? Are you trying to get away from something, do you have a personal problem with Tony?"

Eliza starts sobbing. "Yes, Tony and I broke up."

"What happened Eliza? I don't understand ... but yes, I will try my best to help you transfer to Sydney."

"Thank ... thank you David, I always know I can rely on you for help."

"But what about your property in Williamstown?"

"I will sell that once I know I can get that job in Sydney."

Eliza hates the morning sickness; she feels very sick going to work, but she has to cope.

"Do we have to know anything, Eliza?" Tina asks one morning. "You keep on vomiting. Coming down with a virus?"

"No, I'm fine."

"The whole team is worried about you. Eliza, we are a family — your problem is our problem."

Eliza bursts into tears. "Tina, Tony and I broke up a few weeks ago."

"That explains why you burden yourself working."

"Tina, I'm trying to be strong, not to have another bout of depression ... I'm carrying Tony's child."

"My God, you poor thing ... does Tony knows this?"

"I do not want him to know. Please tell the team that if I transfer to Sydney you won't tell Tony. All your support will give me the courage to continue on living, and I firmly believe I can raise this child on my own, without Tony's help."

"I'm so surprised, David — I never realised this many people would be interested in my property."

"Why not? Your property is in a very good area. Anyway, you can now accept offers for your property — you got the job in Sydney."

"I'm so happy, David. For sure, I can have a new life in Sydney."

"The team will be sad with you leaving, but they do understand. When will the auction for your property be?"

"In the next few weeks, I can't wait."

When auction day arrives, Eliza is so excited and happy — she gets a good selling price for the property.

"Can you manage financially when you transfer to Sydney?" asks Sue.

"Oh yes, definitely — with Celia's money that I inherited, plus the sale of my house, it'll help me purchase a three bedroom house in Sydney. The extra money will be invested in shares and cash."

"That's good to know. Before you go, we will be organising a baby shower for you ... I know it's a bit early but we won't see you anymore. However, distance won't keep us from being in touch with one another."

"That is so sweet, Sue. I will miss you all!"

Special Moments

Each moment
has that special meaning
that will be forever
embedded in our hearts
Each challenge and endeavour
we have gone through
needs patience, hope and perseverance
From each failure and mistake we have made
lessons can be learned
can be used as an inspiration
to start all over again
till we have achieved our dreams.

From *My Innermost Thoughts* by Lorna Ramirez

Chapter 13

The New Beginning

"Good news Eliza! The company will find you a place to stay in Sydney, fully furnished and good for two to three months, until you can move to your own place. I'm sure this will give you ample time to settle in. I informed them that you are pregnant and they don't have any problem with that. They're happy to take you, thanks to your good working record." David continues, "Eliza, how would you be able to cope once you have your baby? Will you be away for a year? They want to know your plan."

"My mum will be coming here to help me."

"That's good. They'll be happy to hear that. The team and I will miss you and your smile, Eliza. You're a beautiful charismatic person. All of us will be sad that you're leaving us."

There's a knock on the door and Marie enters. "Excuse me, David. Can I have a word with Eliza?"

"Sure Marie. We're finished talking. She's all yours."

"Thanks David." Outside the office, Marie says to Eliza, "The team is planning to organise a baby shower at my place. Don't worry Eliza, we will organise everything. You don't have to do anything."

"Wow! That is so sweet, Marie. You don't have to do that."

"We would love to do it, Eliza. Be ready by 3.00 pm. Sue will be picking you up."

"Wow! Not only is our team here but some of the ladies in the different departments!"

"Yes Eliza, it shows how popular you are. I prepared lots of games to be enjoyed by everyone. We're looking forward to when you open all your presents."

"Me too Marie! This will be a fun night. Even the finger food you guys prepared is so delicious!" Eliza is about to cry.

"No Eliza, this is not the time to shed tears. This is the time for celebrating the coming of your baby."

"Of course it is!" Eliza wipes her tears.

"Ladies, it's about time for Eliza to open the presents." Everybody gathers in anticipation.

Excitedly, Eliza utters, "I don't have to buy clothes,

blankets, diapers, baby booties and other baby accessories! I have it all! I will just only have to buy baby stroller and crib. Thanks to all of you guys. I'm overwhelmed by your generosities."

"Oops! No crying again!" Marie reminds Eliza.

"I will really miss you all."

"Where are you planning to buy your house, Eliza?"

"It's a townhouse, Marie. Somewhere in Parramatta. It's a good area, close to the city and near transport, schools and all amenities. Thank you, guys. You're making my life comfortable considering my present predicament."

In three weeks' time, Eliza will be moving to Sydney. Now she realises the work involved in moving. She has to ring up the removalist and the storage company, then pack everything she can carry. She doesn't want to stress herself, and will do it slowly.

Eliza thinks it's good she's busy, enabling her to forget Tony. She supposes that after too many frustrations, heartaches and problems, she's become numb and can't feel any more hurt. Does this make her a stronger person? Her present goal is only to be able to raise her child and be a good mother.

She rings her mum in the Philippines to give her the news. "Hi Mum!"

"Eliza! So good to hear your voice. How are you?"

"I'm okay Mum, but sad to inform you that Tony and I broke up."

"*What?* How do you cope with this? I'm hoping you won't succumb into depression again. My poor baby. So sorry to hear that."

"Don't feel sorry for me, Mum. I'm okay, got over it. I'm stronger now than before. Anyway, for the good news. I'm pregnant and carrying Tony's child. He doesn't know about this."

"... Eliza, I respect your decision."

"Thanks — as always, I knew I could depend on you. How are my brothers?"

"They are okay, still with me."

"Mum, I need your help."

"Anything dear, please don't hesitate to ask."

Eliza continues, "I will be transferring to Sydney in three weeks' time. I need someone to help me once I have my baby. I want to be back at work six months after my baby is born."

"Oh Eliza, I cannot wait to see my first grandchild. I would like to be there soon, even before the birth of your child."

Upon arriving in Sydney, Eliza says to her taxi driver, "Can you please drive me to this address?"

"Are you visiting here, Madam?"

"No, I'm relocating here from Melbourne."

"I'm sure you will like it here. Better than Melbourne, our weather is not as unpredictable."

The villa unit is nice, and completely furnished. Eliza doesn't have to buy anything except food. She makes herself comfortable by throwing herself in bed, sleeping for nearly two hours. Feeling relaxed, Eliza goes to the kitchen to have a cup of tea when the doorbell rings.

"Hi! My name is Edna. I live on the right side of your unit. You must be the one renting the place?"

"Yes, my name is Eliza."

"Well Eliza, I brought you a cake I just baked today. I'm a widow, all my children are all grown up. I have three grandchildren."

"Nice to meet you, Edna. This is my temporary accommodation for three months, then I will move to my own place. I just relocated here from Melbourne."

"So you won't be my neighbour. Well, I don't want to interrupt what you were doing, but if you need anything, just say so. I'm more than happy to help."

"Thanks Edna, sure I will."

For Eliza, having one week before going to her new job is great. This gives me enough time to familiarise herself with Sydney, then she can cope and adjust very well and be more focused with her new job. Eliza wonders if her new manager is as likeable and compassionate as David.

She also thanks God she doesn't have morning sickness anymore.

"I can't believe this is my first day of work and it's a miserable weather. Cold breeze, windy and raining, truly reminding me of Melbourne's weather. As much as my body resisted of getting up, I should be preparing myself and avoid being late for my first day in the job."

At the office, a young good-looking guy welcomes Eliza. "Hi Eliza! I'm Allan Williams, your manager. I've heard everything about you."

"I do hope nothing negative!"

"Oh no! All positive. They all love you and we're happy that you'll be working with us, a loss for your department and definitely a gain for us." Eliza blushes. "Please come into my office to discuss your responsibilities but first, I would like to ask — when will you be having your maternity leave?"

"It will be by December, Mr Williams."

"Just call me Allan, Eliza."

"Okay, Allan."

"That's better."

"My mum will be coming here soon from the Philippines before the baby's born. Returning back to work after six months will pose no problem, Allan. Mum will help me with the baby and I'm sure that will work out just fine."

"That's perfect, Eliza. Actually, we're not that busy in December and early January. I'll hire temporary staff to help us while you're away."

"Thanks Allan."

Allan starts briefing Eliza on her responsibilities and duties. "Now that you know what you'll be doing, I'll introduce you to our team. Like your team in Melbourne, we are also a close knit group here in Sydney — we work as a team in order to achieve our goals and get the best results as quickly as possible. You will cover less critical aspects of the news. Once back from maternity leave, you'll be more active in the field."

"Thanks Allan, and rest assured I will do my very best."

"I know you will."

Allan is happy with Eliza's output of work and promises to promote her. It's basically the same job she had in Melbourne.

"Eliza, what will you be doing after work?"

"Go home and rest. Why, Kathy?"

"Would you like to come with us for a drink or two? For bonding and getting to know you better."

"That's nice Kathy. I won't be able to drink though, and I don't want to be late. I don't have a car yet."

"Don't worry about that. Michael, would you be able to

drive Eliza home tonight? She will be with us at the Bucket List Café."

"Of course I can. And Eliza, you will enjoy our company."

"Thanks Michael. What an unusual café name, why Bucket List?"

"I don't know. I suppose one should experience going in there before they kick the bucket." They all laugh. "Burgers, tacos, great drinks and a nice vibrant setting — and in the heart of Bondi Beach. Quite expensive but this time it's a special occasion, we all want to welcome you as part of the team."

"That's nice. I feel I've been in this team for quite a while already. Now I'm missing my work colleagues in Melbourne. If we're not busy, we go out and bond together."

"Wow! I'm impressed! This is a trendy café with a million dollar view!"

"We do not normally go here. Only once in a while," added Olivia.

Everyone has a good time, sharing stories, jokes and experiences as newspaper journalists. "Well Eliza, don't hesitate if you want Michael to drive you home."

"Thanks Olivia. I'll be going in about half an hour. Really enjoying your company, guys. Thanks for a nice evening."

"Eliza, do you know Michael is single and very negotiable?" All of them burst into laughter.

"Not interested Kathy." They all laugh again. "At this stage, my only focus is settling in Sydney and raising my child. It's getting late, Michael, can you please drive me home?"

"Sure Eliza, at your service."

"Thanks guys for the evening and see you all Monday. Have a nice weekend, guys. Bye and Good night!"

The next two months pass so quickly for Eliza. In the next few weeks she'll be able to move to her place. This baby is getting stronger by the day, kicking most of the time. And in another two months' time, her mum will be here. Eliza feels really proud of herself for coping well. She's more involved with her work and thinking of Tony less and less by the day. He had hurt her so much and she's still very angry at him. He used her as a toy, an experiment. She should have known it from the start, but now feels she was so blinded by her deep love (or lust) for him.

The phone rings.

"Hi Eliza! This is Stella, your real estate agent. Everything is fine, I will be giving you your key next weekend."

"Thanks Stella. Very excited to have my own place!"

"Good luck, Eliza. Hoping you will like it here in Sydney."

On Saturday morning, Eliza wakes up early and goes to the real estate agent.

"There you are Eliza," Stella says with a smile. "Here's your key. Good luck for your new life here in Sydney."

"Thanks, I know I will love it here."

The townhouse is so near with all the amenities, shops, transport and even schools. Eliza is sure her mum will love it here and will settle soon in Sydney. The place is perfect: three bedrooms, lounge room, a small formal dining room and a lovely functional kitchen. She'll name her child Tony but he'll be using her last name, Martinez. She cannot wait for this baby to come out.

At the office, Eliza excitedly tells her team that in a week's time, she will be moving.

"Good news, Eliza. We'll help you. Hopefully we won't have any urgent work to do."

"Thanks guys. Very much appreciate it."

Eliza, now heavily pregnant, is looking forward to the birth of her child. Having settled in Sydney, she's found new freedom and feels happy and content with herself.

"Eliza, are you still feeling comfortable working? When will you be having your maternity leave?"

"Next month, Olivia — so excited! My baby means everything to me and next week my mum will be coming."

"Don't forget to give us a call if you need help."

"I will, Olivia. Thanks for the concern."

"Hi Michael. Can I ask you a favour?"

"Sure Eliza, what's up?"

"Next Saturday my mum will be arriving, can you please drive me to the airport to pick her up?"

"Of course I will."

True to his promise, Michael arrives early on Saturday. "How are you today?"

"I'm okay, really looking forward for Mum to arrive. Hope the plane won't be late."

"Don't worry, Eliza. It's Saturday and I don't have any plans for today. The team will be coming tomorrow, Sunday. We'll let your mum rest first for today. They'll bring food so you don't have to worry. They'd like to see you and welcome your mum."

"So lucky am I to have friends like you guys!"

At the airport, Eliza and Michael don't wait long; the plane landed early. "Welcome to Australia, Mum!"

"My gosh! Eliza, you are big! And who is this handsome guy with you?"

"Mum, this is Michael, my workmate here in Sydney."

"Happy to meet you, Mrs Martinez."

"Eliza, so excited to see you and I'm looking forward to my first grandson."

"You will love it here in Sydney, Mum. The weather is not as cold as Melbourne. And of course, the joy of having your first grandson."

Arriving at home, Eliza suggests for her mum to have a rest and sleep. "Mum, I realise that you didn't have much sleep last night on the plane, so I won't disturb you. You can sleep as much as you want while I prepare lunch for us. Michael, do you want to stay for lunch?"

"Oh no, Eliza, thanks."

"Thank you Michael."

"My pleasure."

The following day, Sunday, Kathy, Olivia, Gary and Michael arrive around 6.30 pm. They bring with them lots of food and drinks.

"Come in guys. Mum, these are my workmates. Of course you already met Michael."

"Thanks for all of you for making my little girl settled well in Sydney."

"She deserves this, Mrs Martinez. Now we know where Eliza got her good looks from." They all laugh.

"By the way, Eliza, Allan won't be able to come due to family commitments. He is extending his warm 'Hello!' to your mum. We didn't bring any alcohol tonight but we still have to propose a toast," Gary suggests. "To Eliza, and her equally gorgeous mum. We all hope you can find happiness in life. Who knows? Probably one day you will have a chance to meet the love of your life. We also welcome to Australia your mum, Mrs Martinez."

"Thanks to you all but one thing is certain, I will just concentrate on looking after my child. My heart is already closed to any man who will try to steal it." They all burst into laughter. Eliza continues, "Deep within I know I can do this on my own. I believe here in Sydney is my new life and a new beginning. Mistakes from my past will all be forgotten and now I'm looking forward for better and happier days ahead."

Yesterday's lesson and soul-searching experiences
Are needed to make the present foundation effective
And stronger for a better and successful tomorrow.

From *My Innermost Thoughts* by Lorna Ramirez

Chapter 14

Single Mum

A knock on Eliza's room. "Come in Mum. I'm already awake."

"Will you be going to work today? It's almost 8.00 am."

"Aaahh. I'm so tired. We had a good time last night. I don't feel like working today." Getting out of bed, Eliza feels something between her legs.

Mrs Martinez screams, "Eliza! You are bleeding!"

"Yes, I am! Mum, I'm so scared. I do hope I won't lose my baby."

"I'll ring the ambulance."

The ambulance comes quickly and Eliza is rushed to the hospital.

"You are lucky you got here in time, Miss Martinez. Your placenta is detaching from your uterus. It is called placenta previa. This is causing the bleeding."

"Is my baby in danger, Doc?"

"No, your baby is safe, but we will be doing further treatment and possibly a caesarean operation."

"Please do whatever possible just to make sure my baby will be safe."

"Do not worry, Miss Martinez. Both you and your baby are in good hands. We will do the operation tonight."

Eager and worried, Mrs Martinez says, "Doc, are you sure both of them will be okay?"

"Of course they will be."

"Mum, can you ring the office today and tell them? I'm taking my maternity leave now."

"I will, Eliza."

"Thanks Mum."

Eliza is prepared for surgery. They give her a regional anaesthesia, a spinal block. It will numb the lower part of her body, while allowing her to be awake for the whole operation.

The C-section takes almost an hour. Then the cry of a baby fills the room.

"Oh, what a beautiful sound," Eliza utters.

"It's a healthy baby boy, Miss Martinez."

The baby is placed on Eliza's chest, and with a burst of emotion, Eliza says, "I cannot believe you are real and so gorgeous."

"Okay, Miss Martinez, it is time to transfer you to the

maternity ward for recovery. Expect to feel very sore in your abdomen, we'll give you medicine for the pain."

"How are you feeling today, Eliza? Did you have a good rest?"

"Not really, Mum. My abdomen is still sore. They gave me medication, at least it helps ease my pain."

"By the way Eliza, your workmates will come and visit you once you are home. Probably in a week's time to give you time to recover."

"That's very kind of them. I know Kathy is especially excited at meeting my baby boy. Mum, in three days I will be released. Can you please ring Michael and ask if he can possibly pick us up from the hospital? If he is busy, we can go by cab."

"I personally think that Michael will be happy to pick us up."

"Mum, the doctor advised me to avoid strenuous activities and no heavy lifting for about ten weeks. Really Mum, I do not know what I will do without you."

"It's okay baby, I'm always here for you."

After three days, Michael arrives. "As always I can rely on you, Michael," says Eliza.

"My pleasure, Eliza. Are you ready to go now?"

"Yes Michael. Mum already prepared everything."

Then the nurse comes in with the baby. Michael says, "Wow Eliza! He is such a cutie. He's got your beautiful eyes."

Eliza, sitting on a wheelchair while holding her baby, says, "Come on Michael, it's hard to see that yet. He's only a week old. I'm ready to go home now."

"Where is your mum?"

"Mum is at the accounts department, paying the bill."

The baby seat is securely placed in the car as per the manual's instructions. "So proud of what I've done," says Michael.

"Thanks a lot Michael."

"The place is so well organised. I'm so impressed, Mum. The room for the baby is so nice. Everything's in the right place."

"Remember, Eliza, you also helped in the decoration."

"I know, but you gave it an extra touch."

"Okay, okay. Both of you should share the credit," says Michael.

"Exactly," Mum says. "Would you care to have lunch with us, Michael?"

"Thanks Mrs Martinez, but I have to go, I'm working on a project."

"Thanks again Michael."

"Anytime Eliza. Just give me a call and I will be at your service."

"My abdomen is still sore, Mum!"

"You would expect that, Eliza. It's only been a week since you have the operation. Just rest as much as you can, okay? It's quite difficult to be breastfeeding. You have to try to do it for the sake of the baby. A breastfed baby is healthier than a formula-fed baby."

"My baby has a big appetite so we supplement my breastfeeding with formula. I'm so happy now and my life is complete with the arrival of my gorgeous baby. I will do my best to be a good mum."

Both the baby and Eliza get stronger each day. At the dinner table one night, Eliza asks her mum, "Would you like me to continue to follow up your application for permanent residency in Australia?"

"This time, Eliza, I would love to stay to help you raise the baby so you can concentrate more on your job."

"That's great Mum, your visa is for a year so there will be enough time for me to follow up your application."

"Thanks Eliza. So you named your baby Tony. Is that a good idea?"

"I think so."

After two weeks, Eliza's friends from work visit her. "We are so excited to see your baby boy, Eliza!"

"Here's the baby, ladies!" says Eliza's mum, holding the baby.

"He is so cute! He is so gorgeous with lots of hair!"

"Thanks Kathy. I know, he is so adorable."

"It's only me and Olivia visiting you because the boys are out in the field for a project. Here, we have something for your baby."

"More clothes! Thanks Olivia, Kathy."

"I would love to hold him."

"It's okay Kathy, you can."

"Eliza, you're so lucky you have this gorgeous son."

"I know, I'm so blessed."

Weeks and months pass by so quickly. Eliza will be back to work soon. "Mum, are you sure you'll be able to cope with the baby without me?"

"Of course I can, don't worry."

"If you like Mum, I can enrol Tony twice a week in crèche. There is one near our place accepting six month old babies."

"No! I don't want my only grandchild to be in crèche. I can manage just fine!"

At the office, Eliza's work colleagues are happy to see her back to work. "Eliza, welcome back! I'm sure you are ready for some action now!"

"Definitely, Allan."

"Good, that's what I want to hear."

After eight months, Eliza's mum is given her permanent residency in Australia, much to the delight of Eliza. She knows without her mother it would be quite impossible for her to juggle work, home and the baby!

"Mum, Tony is becoming more and more like his dad. His eyes, his love-killer smiles. It's all like Tony."

"When your child's old enough, I'm sure he'll ask for his dad. What will you tell him, Eliza?"

"I am aware of that, Mum. I'll have to say that his dad left before he was born and that he'd been killed in an accident."

"I do pray that you and Tony will never cross paths with each other."

"We won't. My workmates from Melbourne informed me that Tony and his wife will be living in the US. Before he left, he went to the office looking for me. I'm so relieved that my workmates didn't tell him of my transfer to Sydney."

"That's good. That chapter in your life is closed. This is the new beginning of your life. Michael is such a nice guy. Is he interested in you?"

"Oh no, Mum! I won't make another mistake of being involved with any man. I'm happy now, free from any commitments. I have loved twice and twice I've been hurt. I do not want to love again!"

Mothers

It's in the Mother's heart
That children can find
Assurance of being loved
It's in the Mother's arms
That children can find
Solace and comfort
But
It's in the Mother's hugs and kisses
That the children can find
The real joy of being loved
And most of all
Of being special and cared for.

From *My Passion, My Calling* by Lorna Ramirez

Chapter 15

Chasing The Dream

Once a year, Eliza's mum goes back to the Philippines for a holiday, to be with her brothers and friends. She will stay only for a month then rush back to Australia to be with her grandson. Eliza has been promoted to a supervisory position.

Tony Junior, now sixteen years of age, is a smart, good-looking and responsible child. Both Eliza and his grandma are so proud of him. He excels in science, maths, physics and chemistry.

"Tony, I'm so thrilled to tell you I received an email from Sydney Boys High School. You got a place for the Special Year 12 Program!"

"Really Mum? So happy to hear that."

"We are so proud of you, Tony!"

"Mum, you work hard enough and I will be doing my best to make you and Nanna proud of me."

One Monday afternoon at the office, Eliza receives a call. "Hi, Miss Martinez. Please do not panic but your son is in hospital."

"*What*? What happened to my son?" Eliza screams. She is shaking and drops the phone.

"Eliza, you are trembling," says Olivia, grabbing the phone. "Hi, what happened?"

"Her son Tony is now in the hospital, nothing serious. There was an accident this afternoon. The bus he was travelling in and a private-driven car had collided. The car hit the bus on the side. As a precaution, her son is in hospital for observation. He received only minor bruises and will be released this afternoon."

"Thanks for calling." Olivia turns her attention to Eliza. "Listen, Eliza, compose yourself. Nothing serious happened."

"Oh Olivia, I know I overreacted but it brings flashes of trauma and depression from years ago when a dear friend died in an accident. If this happens to my son, I will be so devastated."

"Okay, c'mon, I'll drive you to the hospital to see Tony."

"Thanks Olivia, really appreciate it."

At the hospital, Eliza rushes and hugs her son. "Tony,

my son, I do not know what I will do if something happens to you."

"Mum, I'm okay, don't worry."

Eliza is so proud of her only son, Tony Jr, a responsible young man who loves his mum dearly. "Mum, you don't have to work hard. I can get a part-time job to help out."

"What? I do not want you to work — concentrate on your studies and continue to get good grades. That would make your mum happy. We are okay, son. What you can do is help your nanna when you get the time. She is getting old and at times needs help around the house."

"But Mum, Nanna insists on doing everything."

"What are you complaining about, Tony?" says Mrs Martinez, entering the room.

"Nothing Nanna. Just telling Mum that you refuse to be helped."

"Well, Nanna is still strong. I would ask for help if needed. Your mum is right, concentrate on your studies and continue getting good grades." The phone rings and Mrs Martinez answers. "Hello, Eliza's residence."

"Hi Mum, this is Jose. How are you?"

"I am in good health. How's Carlo?"

"He is fine. He got a new high-paying job as an accountant in a multi-national company."

"That's good news."

"Can I please talk to Eliza?"

She hands the phone to Eliza.

"Hi Jose, what's up?"

"Sis, I got engaged last month and we're planning to get married in a year's time."

"Do whatever you think is right, follow your heart."

"I know sis, but Mum does not really like Lydia, my fiancé. I'm quite reluctant to tell her."

"Jose, if you really love her, go on."

"Thanks, sis."

"You and Carlo should visit us here in Australia and spend Christmas with us."

"That's exactly what I'm planning to do, and tell Mum personally about my engagement."

"Tony will be graduating this year from high school. He is busy now studying for his Higher School Certificate."

"Good, we'll be there for Christmas. See you soon, sis."

"Mum," Eliza says, "Carlo and Jose will be spending Christmas with us."

"So happy to hear that, Eliza. Now we'll all be here celebrating Christmas and New Year."

At the end of the year, it's the day that everybody is waiting for: the results of HSC exams. Tony screams at the top of his voice, "I got the top mark of 99.9 in my exams. That would qualify me to enter medicine!"

Eliza hugs his son. "I can't ask for more, that's the aftermath of all your hard work."

"Thanks Mum. I'm quite confident I'll be admitted at the University of Sydney."

"Of course you will. No doubt about it," assures Eliza.

Monday morning at the office, Eliza excitedly tells her workmates about Tony's successful exam results. "Kathy, I think I'm more excited and overreacted."

"I don't blame you for that. What an achievement for your son."

"Thanks Kathy."

It's almost three days until Christmas. Jose and Carlo have arrived in Australia from the Philippines. Everyone's joy can be felt within the family. At last they will be spending the festive season together. A time for bonding for the whole family.

Jose says to Tony, "Wow, you are a handsome guy. It's almost six years since I last saw you. I heard from your mum you did very well in your exams."

"Yes, Uncle Jose."

"Well, that calls for a celebration."

"Guys, do not make a big thing about this. Just all

of us being together this festive season is the best gift I ever had."

"You are such a good son, Tony." Eliza hugs her son.

The whole family has a memorable and special Christmas, exchanging gifts and welcoming the New Year with the usual Philippine tradition of "Media noche" (a meal with the whole family after welcoming New Year). At the dinner table, Jose says, "Mum, Lydia and I are engaged and planning to get married in a year's time."

"Repeat that again, Jose."

"Mum, I said Lydia and I will be getting married."

"Why? Can you not find a better girl than her?"

"But Mum, I love Lydia — it'll cause me so much pain if I leave her. I came here to seek your blessing."

Mrs Martinez isn't smiling. "What can I do? You already made your decision. Okay, you have my blessing but do not blame anyone but yourself if, in the future, you realise she is not the right girl for you."

"I won't, Mum. It won't happen."

"Don't spoil our celebration, Mum," says Eliza. "You have to deal with it. It's what Jose wants." Turning to Jose, she says, "We will support you."

"Thanks sis."

"How about Carlo? Any serious relationship yet?"

"Oh no, sis. I'm busy with my work and no time for girls."

For the holiday season, Tony and Eliza take Jose and Carlo to different tourist locations. The whole family stays two nights at Lorne, enjoying the sceneries and ocean views.

Jose says, "Australia is a nice place to stay but I have no intention of staying permanently here. Both Carlo and I have good paying jobs and friends back home. Anyway, we will come and visit you."

"Thanks. That is nice to hear," comments Eliza.

After three weeks, it's time for both Jose and Carlo to leave; as always, goodbyes are the hardest and most painful moments. Eliza, wiping the tears in her eyes, says, "Look after yourselves. Don't worry about Mum. She is happy here."

"Yes, I'm happy here — as much as I do love both of you, Eliza and Tony need me here more than you two boys." Finally, they hug and kiss goodbye. It's time to go and move on.

Tony is admitted to the University of Sydney. Beaming with joy, Tony says to his mum, "I will be doing my pre-med at the school that I wanted."

"I'm so proud of you, Tony. But you must remember this is only the beginning of a long journey for your dream. You'll need hard work, dedication and perseverance to achieve what you want. The question now is ... are you prepared to do it for a long haul?"

"Don't worry, I'm passionate about this course."

"Well, I am just warning you."

After almost five years as an undergraduate on pre-medical course, Tony is now applying for an internship and residing to a hospital. His hard work and determination to succeed in his chosen career enables Tony to get excellent grades. One time, Eliza asks, "You're almost finished with your medical school. Do you know which hospital you'll go to for your internship?"

"I would like to be accepted at the Royal Prince Alfred Hospital."

"You will, Tony."

"I hope so."

Eliza is now the head of the department and Tony is doing a year of internship. After that, he becomes a resident medical officer at Royal Prince Alfred Hospital. It is required in Australia to complete a compulsory rotation in the emergency department, general medicine and general surgery for at least two years.

"Oh Mum, the emergency is always full on, so busy. Not enough time for doing everything. Sometimes I get so frustrated."

"Tony, you can do only as much as you can. Most of all, you have to look after yourself. Listen Tony, I miss your nanna. Since she passed away, at times I feel empty. I'm so used to seeing her around the house. Her sweet smile and comforting words ... and now Tony, I seldom see you. You're always at the hospital."

"Mum, you should be able to cope by now. It will get worse and worse. After I'm done as a resident medical officer and become a full-fledged doctor, I won't stop there. I will continue training as a brain specialist."

"You still want to continue that, Tony? I'm not getting any younger, I want to see my grandchildren before I'm gone and be with your nanna."

"Sorry Mum, it will take quite a while for that. I still have to chase my dreams before I settle down — and besides, I have not met the right woman."

With sadness Eliza says, "I understand."

Tony is one of the best resident doctors at the hospital. Then his supervisor says, "Tony, please see me at my office around 2.00 pm this afternoon. Delegate what you are doing to others. I want to talk to you on some important matters."

"Yes, sir." Tony is so anxious and terribly nervous that day, not knowing what his supervisor will say. When the time comes, he knocks at the office door.

"Come in. Oh, it's you Tony. Please have a seat. I know you are one of the best resident doctors here in our hospital

— all your work colleagues praise your dedication and quality of work. What is your plan upon completing your residency?"

"Thanks for the praise, Dr Jones. My plan is to do further training and be a neurosurgeon."

"That's great. That's what I wanted to hear from you. It is a very challenging job and the highest in the medical profession, but I believe you will be successful in any field you choose. Of course, you are aware by now you can apply for the Surgical Education Training program that's sponsored by the Royal Australasian College of Surgeons. However, having said that, do not forget to slow down a bit. How long have you been working today?"

"Um ... 16 hours, I think?"

"No, Tony. You had been working for 21 hours. You need to rest. Go home. Re-energise."

"Thanks Dr Jones. I will do that."

By the way Tony, my cousin's daughter from America's visiting and will be going back soon. My wife and I will be throwing a party tomorrow night for her departure. I'm inviting you. You can bring your mum, if you do not have any girlfriend."

"Sure, I will Dr Jones."

"Good. So I will see you tomorrow night."

"Wow, what a surprise! You're home today. What happened, Tony? You feeling okay? Are you sick?"

"I'm fine, Mum. I just want to rest."

"Well, it's about time!"

"Mum," Tony continued, "Dr Jones, my medical supervisor, is inviting us to his house tomorrow night. His cousin's daughter will be heading back to the US after two weeks in Australia."

"Of course I would love to come. It's very seldom we go out together."

"I know, Mum. So sorry for that. I'm so busy at work."

"Will you be still going for training as a specialist as we discussed before?"

"Yes, nothing changed."

"In that case, I will support you in whatever decision you made."

"Thanks, Mum."

Dr Jones's residence is in an exclusive suburb in Sydney Harbour. When they arrive, Dr Jones says, "There you are, Tony. Is that your mum? No wonder you are such a handsome guy. Your mum is ravishingly beautiful and still looking young — she could be mistaken as your girlfriend, Tony."

They both laugh.

"Tony, I will introduce you to my niece Norma. I'll find her." After a few minutes, Dr Jones is with a stunning beautiful brunette lady. "Norma, this is Tony, one of the finest resident doctors in the hospital."

"Hello, Tony, glad to meet you."

"The pleasure is mine."

"Okay, I'll leave you two. I'm sure both of you have many things in common. I will introduce your mum to my wife and guests."

"So Tony," says Norma, starting the conversation, "after your residency, are you planning to be a specialist?"

"Sure, I would like to be a neurosurgeon."

"Wow," Norma says. "That is a very challenging and very difficult branch of medicine. "

"Yes, but since I was a small boy I've been fascinated with human brains and how they work."

Norma laughs. "Really, that's beyond my comfort zone."

"How about you, Norma? What are your plans?"

"Since I love to be with children, I would like to be a paediatrician."

"That's great. I'm sure you will be a successful, gorgeous paediatrician."

"Thanks, Tony."

"How are your parents? Are they in America?"

"My mother passed away when I was two years old and I still live with my dad. He's a professor in Harvard University. My dad never remarried."

"Sorry to hear that."

"How about you, Tony? Your mum is so gorgeous, and where is your dad?"

"My dad died before I was born in a car accident. Mum was five months pregnant. Like your dad, Mum did not get married. We both have the same sad stories, we should introduce my mum to your dad?" They both laugh.

"Nah! Bad idea," Norma says. "I personally think it's destiny the two of us have met but wrong timing, I won't have a chance to know more of you. I'm leaving tomorrow night."

"Well, we can still keep in touch with one another — emailing, writing and other social media to keep our friendship going."

"I'm not promising anything, Tony. I know both of us will be preoccupied and too busy pursuing our dreams. Only time will tell."

"You're right there. But I really meant what I said. It is such a pleasure meeting you."

"Thanks. I feel the same way."

It's close to midnight when the party ends. Inside the car, Eliza says to Tony, "Norma seems to be a nice lady. And not only that, she is beautiful and smart."

"I know, Mum. But at this moment I don't want to have a relationship with anyone until I can achieve what I want."

"I understand, son. It's your life, your choice and your decision."

Tony completes the residency and starts working as a trainee for neurosurgery. His excellent grades and good working record get him accepted into the Surgical Education Training (SET) program. He is already working as a qualified full-pledged doctor and earning a good salary while doing the specialist training. Long hours of work and study make his mum more worried than ever. "Tony, please slow down for your own sake."

"Don't worry, Mum. I'm okay. I do enjoy what I'm doing."

"Alright, I won't worry anymore."

After five years of dedicated hard work and perseverance, at last Tony is a full pledged neurosurgeon. And Eliza cannot be any prouder. "Tony, you finally made it. Now is the time to think of yourself and have a family. I'm not getting any younger. I want to see my grandchildren before I leave this world."

"Mum, I still have not met the right girl. It will come eventually."

After a year of being a specialist, Tony drops a bombshell. "Mum, I will be going to America for further training to expand my knowledge as a neurosurgeon. It will take two years or more to do it. If you like, you can come with me."

"What? Tony, when will this end? I thought you were happy here."

"Listen, Mum. Being in medicine is a never-ending search for knowledge and new technologies. I would like to go beyond what I am now."

"I cannot tell you what to do, son. I'm sorry, I cannot go with you. I also love my job here and enjoy the company of my friends."

"Well, if that's the case, you have to deal with this situation, Mum. Sorry to say I will be leaving in three months' time."

With tears flowing, Eliza says, "If that would make you happy, go on and follow your dreams."

"So sorry, Mum." Tony wipes Eliza's tears.

"I understand. Be careful and do find time to write and call as much as you can."

"Yes, Mum. I promise to do that."

Never Stop

Never stop learning
Never stop stimulating your brain
Never stop believing in yourself
Never stop following your dreams
Never stop doing things
You are passionate about
Continue to challenge yourself
Setting up goals to be an achiever
After all, life is too short
To be wasted

From *My Innermost Thoughts* by Lorna Ramirez

Chapter 16

Twist of Fate

Tony wakes up early in the morning and says to his mum at the breakfast table, "I am so sorry and I know you were disappointed last night."

"It's okay, Tony. If you are happy, I will be happy too."

"Thanks for your support."

"Anyway, when did you apply? Why did you not tell me in the first place?"

"I wasn't sure at the start. I applied through ERAS (Electronic Residency Application Service). They required supporting documents, medical qualification, training and letters of recommendation from at least two of the best neurosurgeons in Australia. I will take part and be a member of a training scholarship at one of the biggest hospitals in Massachusetts. The training will be about vascular neurosurgery, problems of the brain and spinal cord, including brain aneurysms, and all carotid diseases."

"Wow, that's too technical for your mum to understand."

"Ha ha, I do not expect you to digest what I said. By the way, remember five months ago I went to America for a week in Boston?"

"Yes, you said it was work-related."

"Sorry, I lied to you. Actually, I was up for an interview, then after a month I received a letter from the hospital informing me that I was accepted. I'm so lucky to get this far."

"I know, and why not? You are a very special person."

Tony hugs and kisses his Mum. "It's almost 8.00 pm. I have to go. I do have lots of things to do before I leave for America."

Tony's work colleagues are very happy for him and one of the staff says, "Gosh, we will be losing the most brilliant and hardworking neurosurgeon in the hospital."

Tony, blushing, replies in a humble tone, "I'm not perfect, Susan. I do have my own demons."

"No, Tony. You are surrounded with angels." All of them burst into laughter.

It's the day Eliza is dreading: the day her only son will be leaving. With sadness she says to Tony, "I do not want you to go, I don't want to say goodbye at the airport."

"It's okay, Mum. Just have a rest today. Don't worry. I will be okay, and I'll try to ring as much as I can." Eliza hugs her son so tight that Tony jokingly says, "I won't be going forever. I will be back."

"I know."

On Sunday morning, Tony is at Boston Airport. It's a sunny weather with a mild temperature of 22°C, in contrast to the winter in Australia. The hospital is quite near to the airport and by taxi, it only takes ten minutes.

Arriving at the hospital, Tony is guided to Dr Singh's office, where he is expected. "Hello, welcome to Boston. Have a seat, Dr Martinez."

"Glad to meet you, Dr Singh."

"So how was your trip?"

"Very pleasant. Great travelling in business class. Very chaotic and hectic at the hospital."

"I can relate to that," replies Dr Singh.

Dr Singh is the head of the research team. He is in his fifties and is a respectable looking man. He talks calmly but with an authoritative voice, yet he seems accommodating and possibly a nice guy to work with. He thoroughly explains Tony's responsibilities in working within the research department and also as a resident neurosurgeon in the hospital. "Dr Martinez, this will be a hectic and demanding training program, but based from your credentials I'm sure you can cope with it. Do you know that Dr Lee, one of the neurosurgeons who gave you the letter of recommendation for this position, is actually a friend of mine? We both have our residency experiences here at the hospital. And I believe he knows your capabilities."

"Thanks Dr Singh, I will do my best to do what is expected of me."

On Monday morning, 3.00 pm Boston time, Tony rings up Eliza. "Hi Mum, did I wake you?"

"Of course not. How was your trip?"

"It's okay. I was travelling in business class. I got all the rest I needed. By the way, I met Dr Singh, the head of the training program. He seems to be a nice guy."

"That's good news, Tony. Thanks a lot for ringing."

Tony is no stranger working in such a demanding, chaotic atmosphere in the hospital. He enjoys challenges and his quest for knowledge is insatiable.

Weeks turn to months, months to years, until his last year at the hospital arrives. One Monday morning, it's a public holiday in Boston to celebrate Martin Luther King Jr Day. Dr Singh says to Tony, "Some family and I will be going for a three day holiday. I'm sure you can manage on your own. There will be some doctors here to help you. Do not hesitate to call for any emergency."

"I will, Dr Singh."

That night, a man in his sixties is rushed to the hospital with a raptured aneurysm. The staff frantically try to get in touch with Dr Singh and other doctors. A nurse says to Tony, "Dr Martinez, the man should be operated on immediately or else he will die. We cannot wait for the surgeon."

"But I'm not qualified to operate here in America, though I'm already a full-pledged surgeon in Australia."

"We cannot let that man die! Your decision, Doc."

"Okay, prepare the operating table. Call the nurses. We will do it now."

The person has a subarachnoid haemorrhage, bleeding in the brain. A neurosurgical clipping will be done. A cut will be made at the scalp, and a small piece of bone will be removed to access the brain. When the aneurysm is located, the surgeon will seal and shut using a tiny clip that stays permanently at the aneurysm. Over time, it will heal.

The operation is a success. Tony goes to the waiting room to tell the relatives and to his surprise, Norma is waiting for the result of the operation. "Norma, what a surprise! What are you doing here?"

"My dad had a raptured aneurysm."

"So it's your dad. I did the procedure — I had to do it. We didn't want to waste time for other neurosurgeons to come. Time is crucial. Glad to tell you the operation was a success. He has to stay at the hospital for a week or two."

The next day Tony visits his patient and Norma is there at his dad's bedside. "Dad, this is Tony. He did the operation."

"Young man, thanks for everything."

"It's a pleasure and my job, sir."

"As soon as I recover, I'm inviting you for a dinner at my place. I understand you and Norma know each other?"

"Yes, sir. Your cousin was my mentor when I was doing my residency in Australia."

"What a small world!"

Dr Singh called Tony into his office to question him. "I heard the story of you operating on someone with a raptured aneurysm. I know you're aware that you are not qualified to operate while you are still doing your residency."

"I know, sir. I followed my conscience, trying to save a man's life even if it cost my career."

"You made the right decision and I admire you for that. Keep up the good work."

"Thanks Dr Singh."

When Norma's father is ready to go home, Norma asks Tony, "If you aren't busy this weekend, we would like to invite you for dinner at our place. If you have time before you go back to Australia, I will be your tour guide. I want to show you Boston."

"Thanks, I'll find the time. It's my last year, so I'll be requesting a week's leave to re-energise and rest. I've been working non-stop, seven days a week and it's about time to take a balance. Surely my mentor will give me a break."

"That's good news, so I will see you Saturday."

"I'll pick you up at 7.00 pm."

"Okay, thanks."

"This is a nice suburb you live in, Norma."

"Sure is. Dorchester Heights is a home for St Patrick's Day celebrations. It's a predominantly Irish-American descent area, and a desirable place for young professionals. From here you can see central Boston."

"Wow, I'd love to live in this area."

"I'm proud of my neighbourhood. Here we are, my humble abode. The house is not big, just enough for Dad and me."

"You love your dad dearly?"

"I love my dad so much. I'm sure you also love your mum?"

"Sure I do."

"So happy you can make it, Tony," Norma's dad says when they enter.

"Of course, sir. You are so lucky to have such a beautiful loving daughter."

"Yes Tony. Blessed to have her. Hey Tony, do you know that Norma is a good cook? She takes the time to cook everything."

"Dad, please. Don't keep boasting about me."

"It's the truth."

"A very delicious meal, Norma. Even the dessert is so yummy."

"So Tony, when will I be your tour guide?"

"Well, I applied for that week's break in the next two weeks."

"Okay, I'm looking forward to that."

It's almost 10.00 pm and Tony graciously says, "I think it's time I have to go. I really enjoyed the food and your company."

"Wait Tony, I will drop you off at the hospital," says Norma.

"You don't have to do that. I will call a taxi."

"That's silly. It won't take long to drive from here to the hospital," Norma insists.

"Thanks for your hospitality."

Norma and Tony have a wonderful time going to different places in Boston. They visit Harvard Art Museums,

Boston Public Market, the Museum of Science, the Dorchester Heights monument and Franklin Park Zoo.

"Can I ask you a personal question, Norma?" Tony shyly asks.

"Go on, you can."

"Why aren't you married?"

Norma pauses a few seconds and explains. "I was married five years ago. It didn't work out. Both of us were busy and we drifted apart. We didn't have any children. We sold our house and I moved in with Dad. From then on, I've concentrated more on my work as a paediatrician. I do love my work. I'm always surrounded with children. How about you, Tony? You're still single?"

"Yes, I haven't met the right girl for me. I'm also busy pursuing my dream and concentrating on my career. Hey Norma, we do have the same story — destiny did bring us together." They both laugh. "Seriously Norma, I'm so happy to be with you. I've never felt this way before."

"Same with me Tony. But I have my reservations. I'm too scared to be in a relationship and falling in love."

"Norma, this time it's different. Give a chance to open your heart and love again." They both kiss tenderly. "Norma, I will be leaving at the end of this year. This time, give me the honour to invite you and your dad to Australia. I would like you both to meet my dear mum."

"That's perfect. Next year, Dad and I are planning to go to Australia and visit his cousin, your mentor. Then surely we would love to drop by, visit you in Sydney."

"I'm so happy to hear that," exclaims Tony. "Really looking forward to introducing you to my mum." Again, they kiss and hug tenderly. It's the beginning of a newfound love for Tony.

Being in love, we start to
Rediscover our inner self and
The real meaning of what
Happiness is all about.
Finding love is magical:
Moments and precious time
We share with someone we
Truly love and adore
Finding love is priceless

Lorna Ramirez

Chapter 17

Crucial Decision

After nearly three years of hard work as part of the Research Training Program and also as a resident at the Boston hospital, Tony is looking forward to going home. With all the extensive knowledge gained from working in America, his future is well cemented in his chosen field.

"Dr Martinez, you will soon be back in Australia; your training here will give you the edge over others to succeed and be the best neurosurgeon."

"Thanks Dr Singh."

"It's okay, Dr Martinez. I admire your talent and passion as a doctor. By the way, a lady called Norma called while you are at the Emergency Department."

"Thanks, sir." Wasting no time, Tony reach the phone. "Hi Norma, I'm returning your call."

"Hello Tony. You'll be leaving in the next few days, can we have dinner before you leave? Oh my gosh, I cannot believe this, I'm the one asking for a date. It should be the other way around."

"It's okay, I'm about to ask you." They both laugh. "You can choose the restaurant," suggests Tony.

"I have one place in mind," replies Norma. "We will be going to the Boston Waterfront Restaurant. You want Italian or French?"

"Let's do Italian."

"Then we will go to the Sportello Restaurant. It's authentic Italian food. I will pick you up at 7.00 pm sharp."

"Thanks Norma. Looking forward to see you."

"Me too, Tony."

"You are looking especially gorgeous tonight, Norma."

Norma blushes and says, "You too Tony. You are so handsome and charming."

When they arrive, Tony is impressed. "This is a nice place. Thanks Norma." At the table he's quickly serious. "I will be missing you dearly. I'm so busy with my career and you are the first woman who's conquered my heart. But then again, years ago I was already smitten with your beauty, charm and personality when we first met at your uncle's place. So unfortunate we were both busy and our friendship did not flourish. However, I do believe that destiny brings us together. I will try my best not to lose you the second time around."

"Wow, I did not know you have a romantic side," Norma jokes.

"Please take me seriously," Tony pleads. "I meant every word I said."

"Tony, I agree with you. I was fascinated the very first time I saw you. I do hope this will be a start of a beautiful and lasting relationship."

"To us." They toast, and Tony kisses Norma tenderly. "Now it's time to eat. Bon appétit."

"Hmm, truly authentic Italian food," says Tony. "The pasta is al dente and the sauce is to die for."

"Norma, when will you be having your holiday?"

"Possibly next year, around October."

"You picked the right season. It's spring in Australia, not too hot or too cold."

"Please do call once you are in Sydney."

"Of course I will."

"And after a week, can I invite you and your dad to my place to meet Mum?"

"Looking forward to it." Neither of them want to end the night, feeling joy and happiness reign in their hearts.

Then Norma says, "Wow, look at the time. It's getting

late. I have to drop you off at your place. I know you still have to pack up and do important things before leaving."

"You see?" Tony says. "Time goes fast when I am with you. I enjoyed each moment we shared together tonight." They say goodbye to each other and kiss passionately. This moment they can feel they are meant for each other. They both promise to make this relationship last, whatever it takes.

Tony has mixed emotions leaving Boston. He's deeply sad leaving Norma behind, the first woman who's stolen and captured his heart, but also feels joy that he'll soon be with his mum. They haven't seen each other for almost three years. Both of them have been too pre-occupied with their careers.

At Sydney Airport, Eliza anxiously waits for the arrival of his son.

"There you are Mum. So, so happy to see you."

"Tony, I really missed you."

"Me too," Tony replies.

"Sorry I wasn't able to visit you in Boston. We are restructuring and doing a lot of changes. And I cannot travel sixteen hours or more these days. Your mum is getting old."

"No, Mum. You still look young."

"Stop patronising me," his mum warns him. "Tell me

everything about Boston. I know you called me four times a year but that's not enough. I want to hear more."

"I have surprise news for you, Mum."

"Tell me, I'm listening. Two things I hate in life — surprises and goodbyes."

"I know. But with this one you will surely be happy, guaranteed."

As they're driving home, Tony says, "I do like Boston, it's a nice city but Sydney is where my heart is."

"I like what you said," says Eliza. "Here we are, home sweet home. I prepared a quick lunch for both of us."

"Mum, you didn't have to do that. I ate on the plane."

"Oh well, we'll have it tonight."

"Good idea," Tony agrees.

"Have a rest, then you can tell me about Boston and the surprise news."

"So what were you going to tell me, Tony?"

"Just kidding Mum, it's really not a big deal." Tony's changed his mind in telling Eliza about Norma.

"Don't do that, son. I'm so frightened that you'll be telling me you have decided to work permanently in Boston."

"I won't ever do that. I love it here in Australia."

When Tony returns to work at the Royal Prince Alfred

Hospital, the staff organise a welcome party for him. "We are so happy the best neurosurgeon is back."

"Guys, thanks a lot. Really not expecting this."

"C'mon Dr Martinez, you deserve this and we terribly miss you."

In a few months' time, Tony is promoted as the head of the Neurosurgeon Department. He introduces new methods and advanced technical procedures he learned from his overseas training. He is now considered one of the best neurosurgeons in Australia.

Norma visits Sydney in November and calls Tony. "Hi, this is Norma."

"Norma, what a surprise. Gee, time goes so fast. It's almost nine months since I last saw you. So sorry I only had the chance to talk to you twice. Great news, I am now the head of our Neurosurgeon Department."

"Congratulations Tony. So happy for you. I'm calling to tell you we are here in Sydney for three weeks. We're staying at Dr Jones's place."

"That's good news. Before I invite you to see my mum, I want to have an intimate dinner with you this weekend. I'll pick you up at 7.00 pm this Saturday?"

"Yes."

"Mum, guess who called me today?"

"Who?"

"It's Norma — that's the surprise I want to tell you. I met Norma in Boston. I operated on her father's raptured aneurysm. I'm taking her out this Saturday. I've also invited her and her dad for dinner at our place. You should meet her dad, he's still a good-looking man at his age. The wife died when Norma was two years old. He never remarried."

"What's the dad's job?" Eliza asks.

"He is a professor in Harvard University."

"He must be smart."

"Sure is," Tony replies.

Tony arrives on time; both Norma, her father and Dr Jones are happy to see him. Norma's dad jokes, "Tony, you are the son that I never had."

"What, Dad? Do you regret having me?"

"No, not at all. I'm so fortunate having you. Okay kids, enjoy the night."

"Thanks Dad."

"Thanks sir."

Both of them have a wonderful time. Tony keeps on staring at Norma's face. Norma asks, "Why are you staring me like that, Tony?"

"Nothing, I'm just missing your beautiful face. I cannot believe you are with me."

"Well, I'm really here with you, Dr Martinez," assures Norma.

Tony smiles and says, "I'm wishing this night never ends."

Norma is impressed with the classy fine dining: "The food is so extraordinary."

"Of course, the best for a very special lady."

They talk and share each other's experiences. Then Tony asks, "Will you marry me, Norma?"

"Wow, that's quick. Not expecting this." When Tony presents Norma a beautiful diamond ring, she says, "This is too much for the night. Of course, I'd love to marry you."

He kisses Norma tenderly. "Will you stay with me here in Sydney?"

"I'm not sure. We have to seriously talk this over."

"I understand."

It's almost midnight when Tony drops off Norma at Dr Jones's house. "Norma, next Saturday I'll pick up you and your dad to have dinner at my place and meet my mum."

"Yes I know. Really looking forward to that." Once again they kiss passionately and feel the intensity of their love for one another.

The moment of truth; finally Eliza will be meeting her son's only love, Norma. Eliza went to the market early that day to buy all the ingredients she needs to cook for tonight's guests. She is so happy; at last her prayers have been answered. Her son will have a family of his own and grandchildren will be a reality.

Tony doesn't work that day and helps his mum with all the preparation. "You will surely adore Norma. She accepted my proposal for marriage."

"That's great, son. I wish you happiness."

"Mum, I'm so nervous. This is the first time I will be introducing someone."

"I know. I have been waiting for this day to come. Please check whether the roast is ready and ... oh! I still have to prepare the salad. I also hope they would like my leche flan (crème caramel) for dessert. We have everything ready — roast, prawns, vegies and my specialty molo soup (chicken soup with pork and prawn dumplings) ..."

The doorbell rings. "Mum, I will let the guests in, I think they're here."

"Okay. I'm in the kitchen taking the roast from the oven."

Opening the front door, Tony says, "Welcome to my house, please come inside. My mum is in the kitchen."

"This is a nice place, Tony."

"Thanks sir. Just right for the two of us. Mum, they're here already!"

"In a minute Tony, I will be there." Eliza comes out from the kitchen, still holding the roast. Upon seeing the guests, she drops the roast and faints, losing consciousness. Norma's dad is in a state of shock, his face pale. He just utters, "Eliza!"

"Mum, what's going on?" asks Tony. Embracing his mum, he turns to Norma's dad and says, "You know my mum, sir?"

"Yes ... very well, Tony."

When Eliza regains consciousness, she screams at Norma's dad, "Why did you turn up again, Tony! Why bring havoc to my family? I won't let you do it again."

"I don't understand this," Norma cries. "What is this all about, Dad?"

"Mum, is there something I need to know?" adds Tony.

"This is a mistake Tony, you cannot marry Norma."

"Why, Mum? Norma is my world, my whole world. I love her."

"I'm telling you that you cannot, Tony."

"Why?" Tony screams.

"Norma's father is your father. Norma is your half-sister."

"*What?*" All of them are in disbelief.

"Eliza, is this true?" says Norma's father, Tony Senior.

Then Eliza explains. "Remember our last dinner together and you decided not to leave your wife? I did not tell you that I was carrying your child."

"Why did you not tell me?"

"That moment is not relevant to you anymore. You made your decision."

"Eliza, do you know why I did not leave my wife? Because that day my wife informed me that she was pregnant, after seven years of marriage. I felt then I had a responsibility for our child."

"But Tony, what about me? You completely ruined and hurt me. Fortunately with the help of my mum and friends, I was able to pull myself and move on."

"Mum, what about us? Norma and me? It ruins our plans," cries Tony in desperation. "A large part of me would be taken away from me if I lose Norma."

Norma says while sobbing, "Tony, there isn't much we can do."

"But Norma, I do love you so much."

"Wait, there is one thing more all of you should know," says Tony Senior, "especially you, Norma. Before the death of your mum, she confessed to me that she is not certain if I'm your father."

"No Dad, that's not true," Norma screams.

"Norma, listen carefully. I do not blame your mum. She was lonely and had an affair with her personal trainer. That time I was madly in love with *your* mum, Tony — and believe me, Eliza, I was about to tell my wife we were divorcing when she told me about her pregnancy. Norma, I did not do the DNA test to prove that I am your father. I did not want to know that, because I do love you very much. You are my world."

Tony's face brightens up. "So there is still the possibility that you are not my half-sister. Why are you so quiet, Norma, what are you thinking? Aren't you happy we still have the chance to be together? Please, I want your decision."

In a very soft voice Norma says, "It's no use, Tony — I've made up my mind. I don't want to have a DNA test."

"What?" exclaims Tony. "We made plans together. Do not say that. I love you so much Norma, please consider this."

"I've made up my mind, Tony. I'm so scared that the result would show you are my brother. I'll be devastated and the feeling of guilt will forever exist in my heart. I will be equally devastated if my father, whom I adore, will turn out to not be my father. Nothing sexual has happened yet so we can still move on. I was hurt once and the second time will be bearable already. Excuse us. C'mon Dad, we have to go."

"No, no!"

Tony tries to hug Norma. But Norma pushes him away. "Stop Tony, I can't do this."

"Please, please Sir, persuade your daughter to change her mind."

"I'm so sorry son," Tony Senior says. "I cannot do anything — it's her decision."

This time Eliza embraces Tony Junior and says, "Son, in life we have to learn to accept things as they come."

Both Norma and her dad walk to the door and say goodbye. Norma, in tears, kisses Tony on the cheek and says, "I'm sorry Tony ... though I love you dearly, I don't have the courage to continue with the relationship."

Eliza whispers to Tony, "Son, I know how it hurts and how you feel. Your father once hurt me and I learned to carry on with my life."

With desperation, Tony rushes outside and pleads, "No, no Norma, don't do this to me."

But Norma plays deaf to Tony's pleading. "So sorry Tony, I really must go."

Eliza follows and hugs Tony. It's a heartbreaking scene: mother and son both victims of tragedies of love, frustrations and miseries in their lives. Eliza, crying, consoles her son by saying tenderly, "Son, I feel what you are going through. We have to learn to survive and it is breaking my heart seeing and watching you this way."

Tony hugs his mum, "Okay, I will try and learn to accept this heartache and try my best to move on."

Decision

The impact or aftermath
We feel within is more significant
Than the experience we had
Hence the next step
Will be crucial
And you can be the only one
Who can decide
On which road
Or journey of life to follow

From *My Passion, My Calling* by Lorna Ramirez

T H E   E N D

Bibliography

Cowen, P., Harrison, P. and Gelder, M., 2006, *Shorter Oxford Textbook of Psychiatry*, Oxford University Press.

Shreeve, C., 2011, *Dealing with Depression*, Little, Brown.

Serani, D., 2011, *Living with Depression*, Rowman & Littlefield.

Prinz, J., 2012, *Beyond Human Nature*, W.W. Norton & Company.

Benns, M., Smyth, T., 2014, *Mistress*, Random House.

Haltzman, S., 2013, *The Secrets of Surviving Infidelity*, Johns Hopkins University Press.

Lieberman, J. and Ogas, O., 2015, *Shrinks: The Untold Story of Psychiatry*, Little, Brown.

Hull, S., 2011, *The Rough Guide to Boston*, Rough Guides.

Vorhees, M., *Boston*, Lonely Planet.

Harris, P., Lyon, D. and Schultz, J., 2013, *Top Ten Boston*, DK Publishing.

Amthor, F., *Neuroscience for Dummies*, John Wiley & Sons.

Also by Lorna Ramirez

Lorna Ramirez wrote this book so she could share her wisdoms with others. She has been an observer of human behaviour and emotions and has built up her own personal philosophies throughout her life. This book is a collection of her strong beliefs and convictions and offers encouragement and enlightenment to others who may be lost and confused or be looking for some positive advice and assistance. Lorna Ramirez is a woman of strong beliefs in her faith and advocates believing in oneself, perseverance when times are difficult and living in the present.

These original poems and wise sayings will be enjoyed by readers young and old, from any walks of life, for their simplicity and beauty.

My Passion
My Calling

Always chase your dreams
But most of all
Always chase your destiny

LORNA RAMIREZ

This authentic story about a Filipino migrant family settling in Melbourne in 1977 is a fascinating read, as it tells of the emotions, the ups and downs, the government assistance in those days, the practicalities, the difficulties, the sudden change of lifestyle and culture but also the joys of living in Australia in the 1970s, a 'paradise' in so many ways, with great opportunities for a good life.

The wife suddenly is confronted with severe trauma, closely followed by another, a time in their lives when everything appeared perfect. Her near death experience results in new beliefs and understanding and inspires her to write.

About the Author

Lorna Ramirez was born, raised and educated in Manila in the Philippines, attaining a degree in chemical engineering and working as a laboratory manager in a textiles company.

In 1977, with her husband and her son and daughter, she migrated to Australia. She worked as a laboratory technician and a chemist in Australia, only retiring in the year 2000 to care for her first grandchild.

Lorna Ramirez has travelled extensively, gaining much from her interactions with people all over the world and building a strong foundation for her philosophies about life. She loves gardening, cooking and reading and playing the piano. She is also interested in the stock exchange.

She has published two books: *My Innermost Thoughts* in 2014 and *My Passion, My Calling* in 2015. In October 2016 Lorna was one of the recipients of a certificate of recognition from FILCCA (Filipino Community Council of Australia).

Lorna is also a regular contributor for *The Philippine Times* in Melbourne and *The Philippine Sentinel* in Sydney.